Set Sail for Adventure

Stowaway!
X Marks the Spot
Catnapped!
Sea Sick

Ahoy, mateys!

Find more treasure and
adventure with the

PUPPY PIRATES

PUPPY PIRATES

Set Sail for Adventure

Books 1–4

by Erin Soderberg
illustrations by Russ Cox

A STEPPING STONE BOOK™
Random House 🏠 New York

Stowaway! text copyright © 2015 by Erin Soderberg Downing and Robin Wasserman
Cover art copyright © 2015 by Luz Tapia
Interior illustrations copyright © 2015 by Russ Cox
X Marks the Spot text copyright © 2015 by Erin Soderberg Downing and Robin Wasserman
Cover art copyright © 2015 by Luz Tapia
Interior illustrations copyright © 2015 by Russ Cox
Catnapped! text copyright © 2016 by Erin Soderberg Downing and Robin Wasserman
Cover art copyright © 2016 by Luz Tapia
Interior illustrations copyright © 2016 by Russ Cox
Sea Sick text copyright © 2016 by Erin Soderberg Downing and Robin Wasserman
Cover art copyright © 2016 by Luz Tapia
Interior illustrations copyright © 2016 by Russ Cox

All rights reserved. Published in the United States by Random House Children's Books, a division of Penguin Random House LLC, New York. The four titles in this work were originally published separately by Random House Children's Books in 2015 and 2016.

Random House and the colophon are registered trademarks and A Stepping Stone Book and the colophon are trademarks of Penguin Random House LLC.

Visit us on the Web!
SteppingStonesBooks.com
rhcbooks.com

Educators and librarians, for a variety of teaching tools, visit us at RHTeachersLibrarians.com

The Library of Congress has catalogued the individual books under the following Control Numbers: 2014023915 (*Stowaway!*), 2014039406 (*X Marks the Spot*), 2015001153 (*Catnapped!*), 2015014057 (*Sea Sick*).

ISBN 978-0-525-58162-8

Printed in the United States of America
10 9 8 7 6 5 4 3 2 1

This book has been officially leveled by using the F&P Text Level Gradient™ Leveling System.

First Omnibus Edition

Random House Children's Books supports the First Amendment and celebrates the right to read.

Puppy ☠ Pirates

Stowaway!

Wally is a pup with a nose for adventure!

Erin Soderberg

Special thanks (yo ho ho!)
to Robin Wasserman—
this adventure never could have
set sail without you.

For Milla, Ruby, Beckett, Maren,
and my real-life Henry—
the readers who inspired this series and
helped out as junior editors
—E.S.

To my three muses—Lynn, Nate, and
Alissa. And our four cats, who were not
amused by the story.
—R.C.

CONTENTS

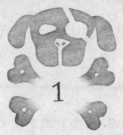

1

Piggly, Puggly, Plop

"Land ho!" Something small, fat, and squealing sailed through the air. It landed on the fishing pier. *Plop!*

A golden retriever named Wally poked his nose out of the shadows. He sniffed. The thing was alive. It *smelled* like a puppy. But it looked like . . . *a pig?*

"Arrrr! Do I smell like treasure?" the furry brown thing snapped at Wally. Her gold tooth shined in the sun. "Why don't ya take a lick? It will last longer."

"I don't want to lick you," Wally said. He backed away.

"Afraid, are ya?"

Wally barked. "I'm not afraid of anything."

In fact, Wally was afraid of almost everything. Sure, he tried to look brave. He held his tail high. He growled. But Wally was the kind of puppy who was only big and mighty in his imagination. In his dreams, Wally lived a life filled with adventure and danger. In real life, he was nothing but a scaredy-pup, looking for a place he could call home.

But he wasn't going to admit that to this gold-toothed *thing*. "Nothing scares me!" Wally growled.

"Nothing, eh? Is that so?" The chubby creature poked her wrinkled snout into Wally's face and yipped.

Wally jumped back.

Gold Tooth giggled. "That's what I thought!"

"What are you supposed to be, anyway?" barked Wally. "A puppy or a pig?"

Before he got his answer, something else came flying through the air. "Land h—*owww!*" *Splat!* It landed inside an open barrel, and

smelly, slimy fish flew everywhere. The creature wiggled out of the barrel and shook her squat body. "Oof! Landing *stinks*."

This critter looked a lot like the first. But she had darker fur decorated with ribbons and didn't have any gold teeth. She was wearing a lacy pink kerchief around her head. Even her *tail* was fancy—small white pearls were wrapped around her curly piggy tail. The pearls wagged as she said, "But did ya see how high I flew? I looked *pug-glorious!*"

"Aye, sister," said the other. "Our cannon launch works! From ship to shore in six seconds flat."

"Cannon launch?" asked Wally, his eyes wide. "Ship?"

The fancy creature turned to stare at him. "Well, well, well! Who's *this* landlubber?"

"Good question, Puggly," said Gold Tooth. "Fur ball here was just asking me if I be a *pig* or a *puppy*." She flipped a fish into her mouth and chewed.

"That's mighty rude. You are obviously a pug, Piggly."

"What's a Piggly?" Wally asked.

"Piggly's a pug," said Puggly.

Wally blinked. "And what's a pug?"

"Us, you scallywag." Piggly rolled her eyes. "She's Puggly, and I'm Piggly."

Wally looked from one pug to the other. "So is a *pug* a kind of *puppy*? Or just a fancy way of saying pig?"

Piggly glanced at Puggly and snorted. "You're not from around here, are ya, pup?"

Wally shook his head. "I came from the farm."

"The farm, eh?" Puggly grunted, wagging her tail so the pearls all clicked together. "You're mighty far from home."

Wally got sad when he heard that word:

home. Because he'd never had one of those, not really. Back at the farm, he had a place to sleep and enough to eat. But it took more than that to make a home. When he'd set out on his journey, he realized he had no one to even say goodbye to.

Wally had been wandering the countryside for weeks. He wanted a life of adventure and excitement, like in stories he had heard. He hoped someday *he* could be a hero and save the day.

But more than anything else, Wally wanted a place to call home.

Just that morning, he had arrived at this city by the sea. It was full of hustle and bustle. Horse-drawn carts pulled lazy humans. Small fishing boats hauled nets full of tasty tuna. Beautiful ships with fancy masts dropped their anchors in the harbor. This place even *smelled* like adventure. Wally had noticed it also smelled like rotten fish and sweat—but mostly adventure!

Wally looked out at the endless, salty blue sea. The ocean was like a stop sign, marking the end of the world. He just *knew* the great adventure he had always dreamed of was going to start here. "I'm looking for adventure," he explained.

Piggly and Puggly laughed so hard they began to sneeze. "Looking for adventure? An itty-bitty pup like you?" Then they turned and waddled down the dock, still laughing.

Wally tucked his tail between his legs. But he knew he couldn't let a little teasing stop him. So after a moment, he quietly followed the chubby pugs off the dock. They scooted under a broken fence and into a hidden alley. The alley was filled with dogs who looked like they were having a party. From behind an upside-down garbage can, Wally listened.

These dogs were loud and wild. They sang songs. They wrestled and played. Wally's ears perked up as the dogs talked of danger on the high seas. Suddenly, everything clicked into place. These dogs were *pirates*. His eyes widened as they told tales of buried treasure and daring rescues. Even in his wildest dreams, Wally had never imagined such wonderful adventures could be real.

As the shadows in the alley stretched and yawned in the late-afternoon sun, one of the pups cried out, "Aye, the pirate's life's for me!"

Wally grinned. *Yes!* He finally knew exactly where he could find the adventure he had been looking for. He howled, "*Arrrr-oooo!* I'm going to be a pirate!"

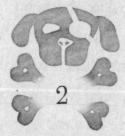

2

The Great Steak Stowaway

The dogs in the alley fell silent. Dozens of glowing eyes turned toward Wally. He peeked out from behind the garbage can. "Oh. Hi. Did I say that out loud?"

There was a long pause. Then every single dog began to laugh.

"A little pip-squeak puppy like you?" a bulldog ruffed.

"A pirate?" barked a tiny, poufy poodle. "You're a landlubber!"

"Lookie-loo, Puggly, it's the farm dog!" Piggly snorted. "And he wants to be a pirate."

"I *will* be a pirate," Wally yipped. "You'll see!"

The other dogs crowded around him, teeth bared. Wally tried to hold his ground, but he was too scared. With the dogs' laughter and growls echoing in his ears, he fled as fast as his fluffy feet would go.

Wally raced to the docks. "I'll show those puppy pirates I belong," he panted. He skidded to a stop on the pier. Right in front of him was an enormous Bernese mountain dog with matted fur, a peg leg, and a patch over his left eye.

Peg leg? Scruffy? Eye patch? It was exactly how Wally had always imagined a pirate would look.

Wally tried to use his biggest voice. "Um, excuse me? Sir?"

The dog thumped and bumped on down the dock. Maybe he hadn't heard Wally.

"Sir?" Wally said even louder, walking along beside the older dog. "I want to be a pirate. Where do I sign up?"

The three-legged dog coughed. "Maybe when you're a little bigger, kid. No kittens allowed on the crew of the *Salty Bone*."

"I'm no kitten!"

The old dog took in Wally's soft golden fur

and his big brown eyes. As the other dog studied him, Wally felt his left ear flop down, the way it sometimes did. "Could've fooled me. Go lick your paws and keep yourself out of trouble. You can thank Old Salt for this advice someday when you're old—and still chasin' squirrels."

Wally didn't care what Old Salt said. He *knew* he would be a great pirate. He would just have to prove it.

So when Old Salt shook his body and trotted away, Wally trailed after him. That was how he found the ship. The masts stretched high into the sky. A skull and crossbones flag rippled in the wind. Pirate crews loaded crates of kibble and cartons of steak onto small wooden boats. Wally heard someone call the boats dinghies. The name made Wally giggle.

But the pirate ship was far out in the harbor. And Wally didn't know how to swim.

Suddenly, he had a big idea. It was brave, that was for sure. But would it work?

He decided a true pirate wouldn't need permission to join a crew. A true pirate would earn his way on board with courage and trickery. A true pirate would get onto that ship any way he could.

And Wally had the perfect way.

The lid on one of the food crates was open. Wally nosed it open a little wider and wiggled in. The smell of raw meat teased at his snout. He reached forward for one quick bite.

Mmmm. *Steak!* A pirate's life smelled super.

Curled into a tiny pouf of golden fur, Wally held his breath and hoped no one would notice him. The lid slid shut over the crate, closing him into darkness. He felt the crate lifting up, up, up—

Fwap!

The crate landed hard, rocking to and fro, as if it were floating. He must have made it onto a dinghy! Wally could feel the little boat moving. His stomach began to feel woozy, but he ignored it.

Wally didn't know much about pirates, but he was pretty sure a true pirate didn't get seasick. A real adventurer wouldn't be scared of the dark. And a brave puppy shouldn't worry about being smushed under the weight of a hundred steaks.

So Wally tried not to get smushed. He tried to be cheerful about the dark. He tried to keep his tummy from gurgling. Because deep down, he was sure he was the truest pirate a pup could be.

And even if he wasn't, it was too late to turn back now.

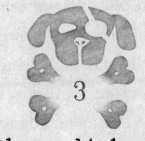

Ahoy, Matey!

"I'm not scared," Wally whispered to himself, over and over. "Pirates have no fear."

Finally, Wally felt the crate being lifted off the dinghy and onto the ship. He heard dogs barking all around him.

"This is the last one," a gruff voice said. Then a door slammed.

Wally waited as long as he could. After many long minutes, he poked his nose out of the crate and jumped to the floor. He was alone in a dark, windowless room full of boxes and crates.

Alone in the belly of a pirate ship!

Wally had never been a stowaway before. But he knew he should stay hidden until the ship set sail. So he backed into the darkest corner of the cargo hold, where he found a dusty burlap sack that would make the perfect bed. It had been a very big day, and Wally knew exactly what he wanted to do next.

He curled into a ball for a nice, long nap.

The boat rocked back and forth. Waves lapped against the side of the ship. As he drifted off to sleep, Wally felt as happy as he'd ever been. Maybe this ship really could be his new home.

When he woke, he sniffed and snuffled. He was trying to see with his nose. Wally could smell food and rats and wet wood.

Then he smelled something else. And he could hear something moving in the darkness.

"No fear," Wally reminded himself. "Be brave."

"Ahoy, matey!" a voice said.

Wally scuttled backward. "Hello?"

"Say *ahoy*, mate." It was a boy's voice. He sounded friendly, but Wally didn't know much about humans. The boy said, "It's important to talk like a pirate if you want to be a pirate. In case you were wondering, the word for *hello* is *ahoy*."

"Oh. Ahoy, then." Wally tried the word in his mouth. He liked the way it felt.

"I bet you're new here, too," the boy said. "You don't look much like a pirate." He touched Wally's fur. "You're so soft and fluffy!"

"Can you see me in the dark?" Wally asked.

"In case you were wondering, I eat a lot of carrots. I have super night vision. It's just what a pirate needs for late-night adventures," the boy explained. "I'm Henry, and I know absolutely everything about pirates. Ask me anything, and

I bet I know it. I'm hiding out in here until it's time for me to make my swashbuckling entrance."

"What does *swashbuckling* mean?" Wally wondered.

Henry paused. "In case you were wondering, swashbucklers are brave, heroic adventurers. Like me!"

Wally sniffed. "And me!"

"But a sneaky pirate really should be quiet, so he won't ruin his mission," Henry added. "So I guess *we* should try to be quiet. Okay, mate?"

"Okay. I'm Wally. Can you keep a secret, Henry?" He didn't wait for the boy's answer. Wally couldn't hold it in any longer. "I'm a stowaway!"

Wally waited for Henry to say something. Anything.

"Henry?"

"Shhh!" Wally felt Henry's hand on his back. "I think someone is coming."

Wally trembled. Henry pulled him closer. Quietly, Henry said, "I think we should stick together. Whaddya say? A brave human pirate and a super-duper puppy pirate? We could make a great team out here on the ocean blue!"

Wally barked, "Yes!"

Henry gently shushed him again and whispered, "Besides, I could use a friend. We can be mates, right?"

Wally had always wanted a friend. He already liked Henry. He nuzzled up against the boy's leg. Suddenly, the air in the room changed. A whoosh of wind, then a thumping sound.

Knock.

Thump.

Knock.

Thump.

Wally and Henry both dashed behind a stack of crates. "Stay quiet!" Henry whispered.

"In case you were wondering, pirates get *really* angry about stowaways. Unless you want to swim back to shore, we can't let them find us now!"

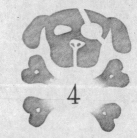

4

Watch Your Tail

Something growled. The growl was followed by more thumps. Carefully, Wally peeked out from his hiding spot.

Two puppy pirates were just steps away. One was Old Salt, the big, three-legged dog from the docks. His peg leg made knocking sounds on the wooden floor with every other step. The other pirate was a small, scrappy-looking Chihuahua.

"Avast!" The Chihuahua's tiny, angry bark made Wally nervous. "Where are all me steaks?"

Wally gulped. He had eaten two or three (or maybe twenty) of the steaks in his crate when he had been in the dinghy.

Old Salt shuffled forward and sniffed. "Somethin' is amiss."

The Chihuahua's body shook with anger. "How am I supposed to cook for this stinkin' crew when they steal me meat?" The tiny dog dashed back and forth across the room. He poked his snout into all the other crates to check supplies, sneezing as he went.

"Calm yourself, Steak-Eye," Old Salt warned.

Wally smelled trouble. He didn't want to wait around to see what Steak-Eye would do next. He had to get out of there. He sniffed in the dark until he found the boy. He nudged his new friend, urging Henry to run, too.

The moment the other two dogs turned away, Wally dashed out the open door. Henry ran after him, his human shoes thumping loudly on the wooden floor.

With Wally in the lead, they zipped down a long, dim hall. Then they trotted up a creaky set of stairs, zoomed through a winding passageway, and rushed past a stinky kitchen. Whenever Wally heard someone coming near, he and Henry searched for a place to hide. They made a good team!

They raced up and up. Just before they hit the open air above deck, Wally screeched to a halt. More pirates were coming!

"Tonight, we follow the setting sun," a scratchy voice ordered. Wally and Henry burrowed inside a pile of rough blankets as the other pups went by. "I've got me eye on eastern gold."

"Aye, aye, Cap'n," answered another voice. "I'm sure you mean *western* gold. Right, Captain Red Beard?"

"Ah, uh ... yes, Curly, of course," the first

voice said. "The sun sets in the . . . ?"

"The west, Captain. As you said."

Captain? Wally thought, his body shaking.
Henry rubbed Wally's ears, and it relaxed him.

They both held their breath, waiting for the pirate pups to pass.

As soon as the coast was clear, the two friends raced up the stairs and popped out into the clear blue sky. The ocean stretched in every direction. It sparkled like it was filled with treasure. Wally could smell the salt water. He heard the flapping of the sails stretched tight in the wind. The cool sea air blew against his body.

Wally was so amazed by the beautiful

view that he forgot where he was and why he needed to be quiet. He barked joyfully. His tail whapped to and fro. It was the perfect moment.

Until his tail went *thwap* against something behind him.

A growl warned him that it wasn't a some-*thing*, but a some*one*.

"Arrrr! What is this?" demanded a scratchy voice. "A stowaway on me ship? You know what we do with stowaways on the *Salty Bone*."

Wally had heard that voice before. He knew exactly who was behind him.

Wally had to get away. But there was nowhere left to run.

Wally and Henry turned slowly and came face to face with Captain Red Beard—who did *not* look happy to see the newest members of his crew.

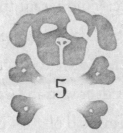

5

A Walk on the Plank

"A stowaway!" Captain Red Beard hollered. "This is unpoopitable!" The scraggly terrier was furious.

Piggly trailed behind the captain. "Aye, sir, you're right. But I think you mean *unacceptable*, Captain?"

"That's right." Red Beard shoved his muzzle into Wally's face. He stunk of dirty socks and fish. "This is unacceptable. Who do ya think you are? How *dare* you sneak onto me ship?"

"I'm Wally." Wally sat politely and offered his paw to shake. "And I want to be a pirate."

All the other dogs laughed. "A pirate?" someone gasped. "You're too soft and little!"

Henry stepped forward and waved at the crew. "Ahoy, mates. I'm a lad of great courage. Where are the human pirates? Because in case you were wondering, I'm here to join the crew, too."

"Human pirates?" the captain bellowed. "Thar be no human pirates here."

Henry looked at the dogs crowding the deck. He slapped his palm on his forehead and said, "Oh, man. Don't tell me I stowed away on a *puppy* pirate ship? Come *on*."

All the dogs behind Captain Red Beard stared.

"Who is this little girl?" the captain demanded.

"Uh, Captain?" said a fluffy poodle by the

captain's side. She studied Henry. "He's a boy."

"That's what I said," Captain Red Beard bared his teeth at Henry. "Who is this little boy? I *don't* deal with humans on me ship."

"He's my friend," Wally said proudly. "We're a team."

"In case you were wondering," Henry said, "I'll be really handy to have on your puppy pirate ship. I have thumbs, and dogs don't!"

Piggly leaned over and whispered, "Maybe if we ignore the boy, he'll go away."

"Just what I was thinkin'," Red Beard agreed. "So . . . Walty."

"His name is Wally, sir," Puggly noted.

"What kind of name is that? Walty it is," Red Beard barked. He sniffed Wally. "You smell like kitten and steak. *My* steak! Are you a spy for our enemies on the kitten ship? Or are you just a thief?" Red Beard snapped, "Pugs! Tie up this scurvy spy thief!"

"I'm not a spy!" Wally said. "I'm brave and strong, and I want to be a pirate. Just give me a chance to prove myself. My boy and me. We'll be a big help. I promise."

"A dog and his boy. You think you can help, eh?" the captain asked. He wagged his tail, and Wally felt hopeful. "I've an idea of how you can help us."

Wally squirmed. "Anything!"

"Well," the captain said, "we've been needin' someone to help us test out the plank."

The other pirates began to chant, "Walk the plank! Walk the plank!"

Wally didn't know what *walk the plank* meant, but he was sure he could do it. He loved walks. "Okay," he agreed.

Suddenly, all the other puppies swarmed around him. They shoved him across the deck. Wally climbed up to a wooden plank that stretched out—

"Over the ocean?" Wally yelped. He tried to sound brave. "You want me to walk on that board over the ocean?"

"Hey, you can't make him walk the plank!" Henry shouted, trying to push his way through to Wally. "Don't do it, mate. You'll fall."

Wally's legs trembled. He looked down

at the shimmering sea. It was a long, *long* way down. He stretched one paw out in front of him and took a small step. And another. He tried not to look down.

Thunk!

Everyone turned toward the noise. It was Old Salt. He slammed his wooden leg against the deck again. Then he croaked, "Wait."

Wally noticed that as soon as Old Salt spoke, the whole crew sat and listened. After the old dog hacked up a fur ball, he said, "This pup might be little, but weren't we all little once?"

"Not me," muttered a huge Great Dane.

The old dog continued, "Maybe he could be useful. Why get rid of him before we find out?"

"What are you sayin'?" asked the captain.

Old Salt sighed. "I'm sayin', let's give the pup a chance."

"But he's a stowaway. That's against the rules!" Red Beard whined.

"Since when do pirates follow the rules?" Old Salt asked.

The other puppy pirates murmured in agreement. They hadn't joined a pirate crew so they could follow the *rules*.

The captain cleared his throat. "Er, as I was sayin', we should give this pup a chance. I was just, uh, *testing* him to see if he was brave enough to walk the plank."

Wally jumped back onto the deck. "Does that mean Henry and I can be pirates?"

"That means you passed the *first* test," answered the captain. "We'll see if you can handle the rest."

Wally's tail wagged happily. "I can! I will!"

Captain Red Beard growled at him. "You better. Or you'll be shark food in no time."

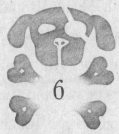

6

Slip, Slide, and Suds!

Early the next morning, Wally stood on deck, waiting for his second test. He was eager to prove he could be a great pirate.

Henry stood nearby. The young boy had stuck by Wally's side all night long, keeping him company in the dark. Wally's new mate talked nonstop, telling Wally everything he knew about pirates. Wally had drifted off to sleep while Henry was still talking. He was pretty sure his new friend hadn't even noticed he was asleep.

"Ahoy!" Piggly waddled across the deck. She snapped a fly out of the air and ate it. "Are ya ready for your next task, lubber?"

"Ahoy! I'm ready!" Wally barked.

"You're gonna be swabbin' the decks," Puggly said, her head held high. Today, the fancy pug was wearing a black lace head scarf and frilly pink booties.

Puggly and Piggly were twins, but they were about as different as two sisters could be. Piggly talked tough and didn't care how she looked, as long as her gold tooth stayed shiny and there were plenty of snacks. Puggly loved anything fancy and ruffled, and she never left her cabin without at least three ribbons in her fur. It seemed like the only thing the two pugs had in common was that they both loved pranks and making trouble.

Wally hoped they wouldn't make any trouble today.

Puggly sniffed. "This place is a stink hole. The captain wants our ship to shine."

Wally had helped clean the barn at the farm before, so he knew about cleaning. "My eye!"

Puggly looked at him funny. "Your eye?"

Piggly giggled. "I think he means *'aye, aye.'*"

"That's what I said," Wally lied. Henry had been teaching him pirate words. But Wally was having a hard time keeping them straight. "Aye, aye, puggy pirates."

"That's more like it," Puggly grunted. "Now get to work." She gave Wally four brushes to strap on to his paws and pointed to a giant tub of sudsy water. Then the two fat pug sisters settled under an umbrella and watched him work.

At first, mopping the decks wasn't too bad. Wally liked the feeling of the water on his paws. He liked slip-sliding around the deck on the brushes. The wind tickled his fur. Henry helped out, too. With his long arms, the boy could get

to all the places a puppy couldn't reach.

But after a while, Piggly and Puggly got bored. That was when the trouble began.

First, the two pugs stepped into the tub of water. They romped and rolled in the tub, splashing water over the edges. Puggly's booties got soaked and her ribbons all popped off, but she didn't even notice. Soon, the ship's deck was soaking wet. And the soapsuds made it slippery.

Wally and Henry mopped as fast as they could. But they couldn't keep up with all the water sloshing out of the tub.

The pugs were having a blast.

"Arrrrf!" Puggly barked. "I've an idea, Piggly." She galloped across the deck and pulled out the cannon launch the two pugs had built.

"*Yo ho harooo!*" Piggly howled.

Laughing and sneezing, the pugs slopped water into the cannon and blasted it all over the deck.

Plop!
Splash!
Squirt!

Piggly and Puggly cheered. They ran in circles. Their short legs slipped. Then—*crash!* They smashed into the tub of water. The whole thing toppled over. Water splashed everywhere!

The pugs rubbed their faces in the suds. It looked like they had beards. Piggly shook her body, and soapy water flew in every direction. Wally and Henry couldn't stop themselves from laughing.

But even as he giggled, Wally knew this was trouble. He was supposed to be cleaning, not making more of a mess! He slid around the deck, trying to mop up all the water.

Puggly yelled, "Don't worry, lad! This is how you're supposed to swab the deck. The sun will dry all the puddles soon enough."

Wally looked up. There *was* no sun. The sky was full of clouds.

"In case you were wondering," Henry said, "this is never going to dry."

Just as Wally realized they were doomed, Captain Red Beard and some of the crew appeared. "What's this?" Red Beard demanded.

"I . . . ," Wally began. "I'm sorry?"

"Aye!" the captain barked. "Ya better be sorry. It's time for me crew's mornin' game of fetch. But you've made a mess of things. Now we won't be able to play!"

Wally felt awful. Even Puggly and Piggly looked worried.

"Please, Captain—" he began.

"You better clean this mess up! You've ruined our fun!" Red Beard whined. "I. Want. Fun. I get fun at ten o'clock and twenty-six o'clock."

Piggly whispered, "You mean ten o'clock and

fourteen o'clock, Captain." She looked at Wally and smiled. "That means ten and two, if you're a landlubber."

"You want fun?" Wally asked, perking up. He faced the captain. "Fun is exactly what I had in mind."

Captain Red Beard growled, "Eh?"

"We were just inventing a new game," Wally said, thinking fast. "Piggly and Puggly and Henry and me. See, it's a new kind of fetch. Slip-and-slide fetch. Watch!"

There was a chest filled with toys on the edge of the deck. Wally trotted over and grabbed a ball, and then he dropped it in Henry's lap. Panting, he galloped across the sudsy floor. Right on cue, Henry tossed him the ball. Wally leaped into the air, caught the ball, then slid— *zoooooooom!*—all the way across the deck.

The other dogs cheered.

"That was some good thinking, Wally!" Puggly whispered in his ear.

"Aye," Piggly agreed, grinning. "You really saved the day."

Wally wagged his tail hard. He was pretty sure he'd just made two new friends.

The puppy crew each took a turn in the

game. Finally, Captain Red Beard stepped up. As he slipped and slid across the sudsy deck, the captain howled, "*Arrr-arrr-aroooo!*"

Red Beard ran back and dropped the ball in Henry's lap. Then he turned to Wally. "Well, lad, it's lucky for you soapsuds are fun. You just passed your second test."

7

Cooking Up Trouble

Wally's next test really stunk.

The captain ordered him to help Steak-Eye make dinner for the whole crew. Piggly and Puggly warned him that it wouldn't be easy.

"If you can survive an afternoon with Steak-Eye, you are one tough pup," Puggly said.

"At least you can't mess up *too* badly," Piggly added. "Nothing could make Steak-Eye's food taste any worse than it already does."

Wally thanked his new friends and stepped nervously into the kitchen. He was a little afraid of Steak-Eye. The cook looked like the kind of dog who might bite.

Steak-Eye glared. "Get your wiggly self over here, lad!"

Wally hustled over to the center of the ship's kitchen with Henry in tow. "In case you were wondering, the ship's kitchen is called the galley," Henry said. Then he took a big whiff and whispered, "And this galley stinks!"

"Tell that boy of yours to close his trap, will ya? Get him outta here." Steak-Eye gave Henry the stink eye.

Wally took a deep breath and said, "He's my friend. We're a team, and wherever I go, he goes."

Steak-Eye yipped, "Suit yourself, ya scurvy dog. But don't let your human get in the way of my supper."

Wally decided to take his chances. He and

Henry were best mates, and best mates stuck together.

Steak-Eye dashed around the kitchen, shoving meat and other ingredients across the counters and the floor. Henry trailed behind the cook, catching things as they fell. Wally watched the cook with wide eyes and tried to figure out what he was supposed to be doing. "Get off your lazy bum and help me out, pup!"

"What, uh, what are we making, sir?"

"Stew!" Steak-Eye barked. "Last night: stew! The night before that: stew! The night before that?" He waited.

Wally guessed, "Stew?"

"That's right! So let's get crackin'." Steak-Eye leaped up on the counter. He dropped things into the bubbling broth with his teeth. Then he peeked his snout over the edge of the pot and lapped up a taste.

"In case you were wondering," blurted Henry,

"you're not supposed to lick someone else's meal. It spreads germs. Germs are not for sharing."

"In case *you* were wonderin'," Steak-Eye said in a Henry-like voice, "you should mind your own business."

Wally pushed Henry toward the stove, and the two of them got to work. Henry dropped potatoes into the stew and stirred. Wally stomped on a piece of meat to try to soften it. Steak-Eye grumbled and shouted and knocked

things over with his crazy tail. Wally chased
after the grumpy cook, trying to be helpful.

When Wally reached down to grab a piece
of fat that Steak-Eye knocked onto the floor, he
spotted an open can of food under the counter.
Wally sniffed it. He decided it smelled yummy.
Wally nosed the can of food toward Henry, who
dumped it into the stew and stirred.

The puppy pirates all arrived in the dining
room a few minutes later. The stew was served,

and Wally thought he had done an okay job during his test.

Suddenly, Steak-Eye yipped. It sounded like he'd been hurt. Wally turned and saw the cook staring at the empty can on the counter. "What have you done?" Steak-Eye asked, pushing the can toward Wally.

"I helped make the stew tasty?" Wally suggested.

Steak-Eye growled, long and low. "You dumped *this can* in me stew?"

Wally lay on the floor and hid his face between his paws. He looked at Henry. Henry picked up the empty can. He read, "Kitty Kibble. *Yum, yum!*" He peeked at Wally. "Uh-oh, mate. In case you were wondering, this is *cat food.*"

"That's right, pup. *Cat food.*" Steak-Eye was too angry to yell. For the first time, the kitchen was silent and still. Strangely, so was the dining hall. Steak-Eye trotted over to the door of the dining room. Usually, the other pirates groaned and whined all through dinner. They loved to complain about Steak-Eye's terrible food.

But today, the only sound was dogs eating— happily.

Wally stood beside Steak-Eye and looked out at the crew. Piggly pulled her snout out of her bowl and cheered, "This is the best stew you've ever made, Cook!" She ran to the kitchen for seconds.

"Pug-glorious!" agreed Puggly.

"Whatever you did, keep it up," added Captain Red Beard.

Steak-Eye did a victory lap around the dining hall. He bowed and trotted across the tables. Then he nudged Wally into a corner of the kitchen and whispered, "The crew can never know!"

"About the cat food, you mean?" Wally asked.

"Shhh!" Steak-Eye growled. "About the 'secret ingredient.' They can *never know*. Do we have a deal?"

"Deal," Wally said. He put out his paw, and Steak-Eye patted it. The mean old cook actually looked happy when he said, "Then congratulations, ya scurvy dog. You just passed your third test."

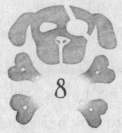

8

Last-Chance Climb

It was time for one final test. After their stew, the whole puppy crew gathered on the ship's deck. Everyone knew Wally had helped make the delicious dinner. Puppy after puppy thanked him for the tasty food. Piggly rubbed her belly happily. "I don't know what you did in there with Steak-Eye," she said, "but I sure hope you stick around and keep doing it."

Wally couldn't believe he had made so many

new friends. It seemed like everyone on the ship wanted him to join the crew.

Everyone, that was, except Captain Red Beard. The captain glared at his band of pirates. "Time to watch little Walty fail," he announced.

Wally tried to look brave and ready. He was having so much fun as a pirate. The ship had sailed far out into the ocean. He had overheard the first mate say they were on their way to a secret island in the middle of the sea. There were rumors of buried treasure. Wally wanted to be a part of the crew who got to dig for it. He wanted to stay here, with all his new friends. He wanted the ship to be his forever home.

He couldn't fail now! "I'm ready, Captain," he barked.

"So far, Walty, you have proven to be an okay pirate," Red Beard said. "Now we test your true strength and bravery. If you succeed, you and your boy can stay. If you fail? Padoodle. Squat. Finaminto."

Wally cocked his head. "Excuse me, sir?"

Piggly looked sad. She explained, "What he means is, if you fail, you're finished."

"That's what I said!" Red Beard complained. He barked for attention. "For his final test, Walty the stowaway pup will . . ."

Piggly and Puggly ran around the deck. Their paws made a *rat-a-tat-tat* sound like drums. Wally felt like they were cheering him on.

". . . climb to the top of the mast and take his turn in the crow's nest!" the captain growled. "If he can do that, I'll think about makin' him a part of me crew."

Wally stepped toward the skinny rope ladder that stretched up the ship's huge mast. He looked up.

Way, way up.

At the top of the mast was a tiny little platform the pirates used as a lookout perch. Wally had seen some of the strongest dogs on the ship run up that ladder. But Wally was different from those dogs—he wasn't strong, and he wasn't big. And he was afraid of heights more than anything else.

He crept toward the ladder. As he put his

front paws on the rope, Henry ruffled his fur and scratched behind his ears. "In case you were wondering, the crow's nest is really high. Looks pretty scary to me."

Henry's words didn't help. Wally gulped. He looked at the captain. "Would it be okay if I take a second to . . . um, stretch?"

Captain Red Beard glared at him. "Fine."

Wally dashed to the other end of the ship and stared out at the endless blue sea. He hung

his head low. This was it: He would fail the test. He would get kicked off the ship. He would never, ever be a pirate. And all because he was afraid.

He was about to tell the captain that he couldn't do it, when he felt a paw on his back. Nubby fur brushed against his side. Old Salt had followed him.

Old Salt was the oldest and wisest pirate on the ship. He didn't talk much, but when he did, it was worth listening to what he had to say. So that was what Wally did.

Old Salt cleared his throat. "Once, long ago, I was a young puppy, too. No one thought I would make it as a pirate. But I proved 'em all wrong." The old pirate coughed. "Ya can't judge a puppy by his spots. I've been around long enough to know how to look deeper. And when I look at you, kitten, I see a pirate."

Wally stared up at the old dog and said, "But I'm afraid. Aren't pirates supposed to be brave? A good pirate shouldn't be afraid of anything."

"Bein' brave isn't about having no fear," Old Salt said. "It's about bein' afraid of what you have to do and doing it anyway. You just have to believe you can do it, and you have to want it. Look deep in your heart, and decide what you really want."

Wally thought about what Old Salt said. He knew what he wanted. He wanted to be on the pirate crew—really, *really* wanted it, more than he'd ever wanted anything. He wanted this ship to be his home. Wally took a deep breath. "I'm ready," he said. "*Yo ho harooo,* let's climb the mast!"

"In case you were wondering, mate?" Henry said as Wally padded back toward the mast. "I think you're perfect for the crow's nest. You're little, and you're fast. That's just what you need to get up there lickety-split."

Wally remembered that he wasn't the only one who wanted to stay on this ship. Henry needed him to pass this test. He wasn't going to let his best friend down!

And Henry could be right, Wally realized. Little and fast might be perfect for this task! He stopped a few feet away from the rope ladder and looked all the way up to the top. It was as scary as ever—but maybe that was okay. Maybe he could be scared . . . and do it anyway.

Wally put his head down and ran.

He ran straight at the rope ladder, as fast as his little paws would carry him. This time, he didn't stop at the bottom. Wally dashed up, up, up. Within seconds, he was at the top!

The view from the crow's nest was beautiful. He hardly even noticed he was up so high, since

there was so much to see. Seagulls dove and flapped around him. Salty air filled his nose. To the west, the other ship sailing their way looked mighty and—

Wait! "Another ship?" Wally said, his eyes wide. He barked as loudly as he could. "Shiver me timbers! There's another ship coming from the west!"

Below him, the other puppies looked like specks on the deck. But Wally could see Piggly peer through a spyglass.

"The pup's right!" Piggly yelped in alarm. She could see the other ship's flag through the lens. "Enemy off the starboard bow—the *Nine Lives* ship approaches!"

Captain Red Beard snapped into action. "All hands on deck. Prepare for battle!"

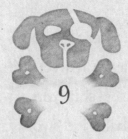

9

Battle Splash

"Battle?" Wally whispered. "Battle!" He dashed down the rope ladder. Henry and the pugs were waiting for him at the bottom.

"The kitten pirates are our worst enemies," Puggly explained. "This is our part of the sea, and they're not welcome here."

"What are we going to do?" Wally asked.

Henry kneeled down so he was face to face with Wally. "Mate, there's danger on the horizon—we need to fight!"

Piggly nodded. "It's true. Those cats will stop at nothing."

Wally was too excited to be afraid. He was about to experience his very first pirate brawl. Around him, the ship came to life. Puppies readied cannonballs and swords.

"In case you were wondering, mates, it only takes one direct cannon hit to sink a whole ship!" Henry was trying hard to take over, since he was sure he knew everything about pirate battles. But no one had time to listen.

When the enemy ship was within shouting distance, Red Beard yelled out a warning. "Avast! We will stop at nothing to keep you old fur balls out of our waters!"

The kitten captain called back, "Aw, go take a nap, ya scurvy dogs. Ya don't scare us. *Hiss!*"

Wally tried to stay out of the way. That was how he noticed someone else was staying out

of the way, too—Old Salt. The old dog sat quietly at one end of the deck, watching as the crew prepared to fight.

Wally trotted over to stand by his side. "Isn't this exciting?"

Old Salt lay down on the deck. The old dog looked unhappy. "Fights between pirates never end well," he said.

"What do you mean?" Wally asked. "Aren't pirates supposed to be great fighters?"

"Great fighters, yes," said Old Salt sadly. "Too great. When two pirate ships fight each other, it's trouble. If it comes to a real fight, there's a good chance both ships will be smashed to smithereens."

"Smithereens?" Wally asked.

"That means pieces. Bits," Old Salt grumbled. "But there's no way to stop this lot from fighting. Captain Red Beard will never surrender, and cats are famous for being stubborn."

Wally thought for a moment. "What if we could figure out a way to make the cats go away without fighting?"

"There's no way to do that," growled Old Salt.

"I might have an idea," Wally said in a small voice. He told Old Salt what he was thinking.

Old Salt looked pleased. "'Atta boy, li'l pirate. That's quite a plan. What do you need me to do?"

"Can you keep the two crews from fighting for just a bit longer?" Wally asked. "I need a few minutes to get everything ready."

Old Salt nodded. "If there's one thing no cat can resist, it's the chance to prove she's smarter than a bunch of dogs. I've got an idea." He thumped across the deck and tried to get the other captain's attention. "Hey, kitty litter!"

The kitten captain leaped onto the rail of the *Nine Lives* and hissed, "What do ya want? Are ya ready to surrender?"

"No, but we've got a riddle for ya. No one on our ship has been able to figure it out. If ya want a chance to prove you're smarter than a dog, solve it for us." Old Salt thought for a long

while. Then he shouted out his riddle: "I am something that's both big and small ... sometimes a color, but at other times no color at all. What am I?"

Captain Red Beard barked and turned to his crew. "Come on, come on ... what is it? Ooh! Ooh! I know! Spit."

Old Salt nudged the captain and murmured, "You're not supposed to be *solvin'* the riddle. I'm just tryin' to buy us some extra time."

Captain Red Beard looked sad. "I'm not supposed to solve the riddle? But I like riddles."

Piggly and Puggly both opened their mouths and drooled on the ship deck. "My spit is clear," announced Puggly.

Piggly said, "Mine's orangeish. But that's because I just ate some cheese."

Old Salt gritted his teeth. "The answer is not spit."

While Piggly, Puggly, and the kitten pirates kept trying to solve the riddle, Wally told the rest of the crew his idea. "How do cats feel about water?" he asked.

Red Beard yelled, "They *love* it!"

"Um," Wally said, "I think you mean they *hate* it, right, Captain?"

Red Beard noticed that the rest of the crew was nodding. "That's what I said. They hate it."

"Okay," said Wally. "So if they hate getting wet, what if we blast them with *water* instead of weapons?"

The crew stared at him. Wally squirmed.

"And how are we supposed to do that?" growled Red Beard.

"Piggly and Puggly's cannon launch," Wally barked. "It's powerful enough to blast the pugs from ship to shore in six seconds flat. Surely it can shoot water from the *Salty Bone* all the way to the *Nine Lives!*"

Red Beard looked confused at first. But soon, the captain's tail began to wag. Then he said, "That idea is just crazy enough to work! Lead the way, Walty. And don't fail us now, pup— me whole crew is depending on you."

10

Pirate or Plank?

As the crew worked together to get the cannon into place, they sang pirate songs. For the first time in his life, Wally felt like he was a part of something important. But even better, he wasn't just a *part* of this exciting adventure—he was *leading* it!

The kitten captain was still busy trying to work out Old Salt's riddle. "Is it . . . a butterfly wing? A cat claw?"

Old Salt laughed. "Not even close."

The kitten captain hissed, "Give us a clue, fleabag. Is it something in the ocean?"

Old Salt looked around the deck and saw that the puppy pirates were almost ready with the cannon. A little clue couldn't hurt. "I guess you could say that."

While the cats continued to guess, Henry, Wally, and the rest of the crew worked together to fill the pugs' cannon with water. Henry proved very useful. Using his strong hands, he lowered a rope pulley over the edge of the ship's rail, then pulled up full buckets of water. The rest of the crew pushed the buckets to the cannon and dumped them in.

Suddenly, the kitten captain shrieked and said, "I've solved your riddle, ya fools!"

At that exact moment, Puggly ruffed, "The cannon is full!" With Wally and Henry at the center of everything, the puppy pirates took aim.

The kitten captain pointed a paw at the

sparkling blue sea. "What's big and small and both a color and clear? Ha! The answer is water!"

"Indeed it is," Old Salt barked. He pounded his wooden leg on the dock. "That be the answer . . . and now here it comes!"

The puppy pirates' cannon blasted out a powerful shot of water. It arched up into the air between the two ships, and then it rained down on the kitten pirates. The kittens all shrieked and hissed and ran for cover.

Before the cannon was totally empty, the kitten ship had turned and set sail at full speed—away from puppy pirate waters!

"Hip, hip, hooray!" the whole puppy pirate ship howled and barked. Henry took Wally's paws in his hands, and they danced around the deck. Piggly and Puggly rolled and tumbled and laughed. Steak-Eye brought out a platter of snacks for everyone.

After a few minutes of celebration, Captain Red Beard barked for silence. When he had everyone's attention, he turned to Wally. The captain looked very serious. "Here, Walty."

"Aye, aye, Captain!" Wally stepped forward. His tail twitched nervously. Was the captain mad at him?

"Sit!" barked the captain.

Wally sat.

"Good boy. Now I hope you realize that I'm the one in charge on this ship," Red Beard said in his angry, scratchy voice.

"Yes, sir," agreed Wally.

"Yet ya thought it would be a good idea for you—a tiny, stowaway pup—to try to take charge of the battle?"

Wally gulped. Just a moment before, he was on top of the world. He had felt like a hero. He thought he had helped to save the day. But now it seemed like he was in big trouble! Wally said nothing.

After a long silence, Captain Red Beard ordered, "It's time for you to step up on the plank, boy."

All the other puppy pirates were silent. Wally trotted across the deck and climbed up the short set of stairs that led to the plank.

"What are you doing, mate?" Henry cried in alarm. "We're supposed to stay together."

But Wally knew he had to do this alone. He looked over his shoulder—at the friends and crewmates he'd come to love during his time as a pirate. Puggly pawed nervously at her ribbons. Piggly gave him a tiny tail wag. Steak-Eye winked. And Old Salt gave him the kind of smile that made him feel like maybe everything would be okay.

Somehow.

Wally couldn't put it off any longer. He leaped up onto the plank. The ocean was *very* far down.

He took one small, trembling step along the plank. Then another. But before he could go any farther, the captain yelled, "Now, young pup, it's time for you to turn and take a bow! You proved yourself today. You belong with us here on the *Salty Bone*."

Wally turned slowly and faced the crew. He bowed, his tail wagging madly. Everyone gathered below him began to sing, *"For he's a jolly good pirate, for he's a jolly good pirate, for he's a jolly good piiiii-rate!"*

Henry rushed to join his puppy friend. "See, mate? You're not going anywhere. Neither of us are." Henry put his hands over his ears and frowned. "And in case you were wondering, mate? Puppy pirates really can't sing." Wally's tail whapped to and fro against his friend's leg.

Captain Red Beard stepped forward with a black bandanna clutched in his teeth. He said, "A pirate's life is filled with danger. You never know what might happen next. But the adventures are many, and the rewards are great." He dropped the bandanna at Wally's feet. "You were a real hero today. I'd love to have you join me crew as a cabin boy, Walty. Your human can

stick around, too, if you want."

"You're made for this life," Old Salt added.
"You should be proud of yourself, kid."

Wally *was* proud. And he was happier than
he'd ever been. With his best mate, Henry, by

his side, Wally stood at the center of all the
puppy pirates and howled.

He couldn't wait to find out what their next
adventure would be!

X Marks the Spot

Every pup loves to dig for buried treasure!

Erin Soderberg

For Michelle Nagler, a treasure
of an editor
—E.S.

CONTENTS

Pug Pranks

Drip.

Drip.

Splat!

Little drops of something wet rained down on Captain Red Beard's desk. The scraggly terrier looked left, then right, then down. He was trying to find the leak in his cabin.

The only place he didn't look? *Up.* So he didn't see the two naughty pugs peering down at him through a hole in his ceiling.

Above the captain, Puggly scolded her sister, "Put your tongue back in your mouth, Piggly! You're droolin' on the captain. If he sees us up here, we're done for!"

Piggly and Puggly loved to make mischief. They also loved to spy. The two pugs had been working on digging open a spy hole above the captain's quarters for months. They had finally broken through. And just in time, too! The puppy pirate captain was having an important meeting with his first mate, Curly. And the pugs planned to hear every word of it.

Wally, a cuddly golden retriever, squeezed in for a closer look. "What if they catch us?" he whispered, peering down at Curly and the captain.

Wally and his best mate, a human boy named Henry, were the newest members of the puppy pirate crew. They had worked hard to convince Captain Red Beard to let them stay on board the ship. Wally didn't want him to change his mind!

"In case you were wondering, it's my turn," Henry said, pressing his face to the hole. "I don't see any maps."

"Shhh," Wally said, nuzzling his wet nose into Henry's shoulder.

Wally and Henry loved everything about being pirates—fighting the enemy kitten ship, joining in on daring adventures, singing pirate songs, and all the great friends they had already made. Wally whispered, "I don't want to get in trouble with Captain."

"Aw, quit your worryin'," said Piggly, her gold tooth glinting. "Do you wanna get the map, or don'tcha?"

Wally did. He had never seen a real treasure map. And this map was drawn by the most famous puppy pirate in history, Growlin' Grace! Many years ago, the fierce pirate captain had buried her pirate booty on an island called the Boneyard. Right after she'd buried her loot, Growlin' Grace had disappeared . . . along with the one and only map to the treasure.

After years of searching, Captain Red Beard had finally gotten his paws on the famous map! So now the puppy pirates were on course for the Boneyard—and the greatest treasure hunt of all time.

Wally and Henry wanted to get a look at the map *before* they landed on the island. And Piggly and Puggly were happy to help. Especially since spying was involved.

Puggly's curly tail wagged. Fancy pink beads swished to and fro, swatting Wally in the face. Puggly loved to get dressed up, even when she was in the middle of making mischief. "Here's the plan, mates," Puggly whispered. "See that metal box on the captain's desk? That's where the treasure map is hidden. Piggly and I have the perfect way to get it."

"Arrrrf!" agreed Piggly. She showed them a horseshoe-shaped magnet hanging from a long cord. "See this? It sticks to metal like glue. We'll have the map in our paws in no time." Piggly gripped the cord between her teeth. Very carefully, she lowered the magnet through the spy

hole. Wally and Henry held their breath.

Down, down, down the magnet went— straight into the captain's quarters. It hung a few feet over the captain's desk.

"Did you hear something?" Captain Red Beard growled, his ears alert.

Wally, Henry, and the pugs froze. The captain and Curly were both sitting on plaid cushions in front of Red Beard's desk. If either of them looked up, they would see the magnet hanging from the cord. And if they followed the cord all the way up to the spy hole, they would spot the spies.

And that would mean *big* trouble.

"I don't hear anything, Captain," Curly yipped. "Let's focus. We have to come up with a plan."

Wally sighed with relief. Quietly.

The magnet dangled over the desk. Piggly

grunted. "Heavy," she growled. She wiggled her chubby body and tried to get a better grip with her teeth. "The magnet . . . it be heavy!" Suddenly, the cord holding the magnet dropped from between her teeth.

Like a snake, the cord wriggled through the spy hole. Henry grabbed for it and caught it just in time. Piggly nosed forward and grabbed for the cord with her teeth again.

But then Captain Red Beard jumped up and grabbed hold of the other end! The captain bit down hard on the cord and tugged.

Piggly didn't want to let her magnet go. It was too useful for pranks. So she tugged harder.

Back and forth the pups tugged. The floorboards underneath the spies creaked and groaned.

"Uh, I don't think that's a good sound," Henry said. "Maybe you should let go."

That's when the captain gave one last, furious yank on the cord. The floorboards moaned louder than ever.

Then they snapped.

Piggly, Puggly, Henry, and Wally all toppled through the hole in the floor and landed in a heap. Right on the captain's desk.

Captain Red Beard growled at the intruders.

"Ahoy," squeaked Wally.

The captain glared. In a scratchy voice he barked, "Avast! What are ya scurvy dogs doin' in me quarters?"

"Spies!" yipped his first mate in her tiny voice. Curly was a puffy white mini poodle who looked as fierce as a piece of lemon meringue pie. But she was the smartest, toughest pup on board. "Someone ought to keep you pugs on a leash. You're nothin' but trouble."

"Sorry, Captain," murmured Puggly. She

smiled under her foofy pink hair bows. "We just wanted a peek at the treasure map."

The captain and Curly looked at each other. Then Red Beard popped open the metal box on his desk. He sighed and laid his head on his paws. "Go ahead and have a look." The group all crowded around the map. "But a look's not gonna be worth much. Because Growlin' Grace's treasure map . . . is blank!"

Magic Map

"Blank?" barked Puggly.

"But—but that's impossible!" yipped Piggly. "How will we find Growlin' Grace's treasure if the map is blank?"

Captain Red Beard scratched behind his ear. "That's what Curly and I were tryin' to figure out." He nosed the map into the middle of his desk. Except for the words GROWLIN' GRACE'S GREATEST TREASURE at the top, the rest of the old yellowed paper was empty.

Wally felt his hopes sink. His first-ever treasure hunt was doomed already.

Henry leaned forward and squinted at the blank piece of parchment. "In case you were wondering, pirates used to draw their maps in invisible ink. Maybe if we hold the map up to something hot, like a candle, the ink will reappear."

The puppy pirates all stared at him. Red Beard was the first to laugh. "Invisible ink? That sounds like hoogly-boogly magic."

"Rubbish," agreed Curly.

Wally took a nervous breath, then said, "Excuse me, Captain? Henry knows everything there is to know about pirates. Maybe we should try it, just to see?"

Captain Red Beard looked uncertain. "What say you, Curly? Do we take advice from little Walty's boy?"

Curly sniffed. "I suppose it can't hurt."

The captain nosed the paper toward the drippy candle on his desk. Forgetting that paper and fire don't go well together, he pushed it a bit too close to the candle. The edge of the paper began to smoke, then burn. Piggly leaped forward and snagged the map, pulling it away from the candle. Puggly stomped on it, just before the whole page would have gone up in flames.

"Uh, Captain, maybe we should let Henry try," Wally said. "Since it was his idea."

The captain grumbled and scowled, but he agreed to let Henry give it a try.

Henry made sure to hold the map a couple of inches *over* the flame, so it couldn't catch fire. As the paper heated up, dark symbols and letters began to appear.

"Shiver me timbers, it's a miracle," said the captain.

Just as the final lines on the map came into view, the whole ship rumbled and shook. It felt like they'd hit something!

"Iceberg!" screamed Captain Red Beard. "Abandon ship!" He dove under the desk and hid his head beneath his paws.

The other dogs looked at him strangely. "Captain?" said Curly. "Sir, we're in the South Seas. There *are* no icebergs."

Red Beard poked his nose out from beneath

the desk. "Of course there are no icebergs. I knew that." Then he yelped in alarm. "Sea monster? I think we're being attacked by the Sea Slug!"

From above decks, someone hollered, "Land ho! The bounty of the Boneyard awaits!"

Captain Red Beard yipped gleefully. "It's just like I said: we're here!" He bounded out of his hiding place. "Yo ho haroo—Boneyard, here we come!"

The captain dashed through the narrow halls and up to the main deck of their ship, the *Salty Bone.* The other puppies raced behind him. In all the excitement, Wally was the only one who remembered Growlin' Grace's map. He nudged it toward Henry, who tucked the map into one of his giant pockets for safekeeping. Then he stuck the pugs' magnet in there, too.

Just in case.

The puppy pirates lowered the long wooden platform that stretched between the huge ship and the sandy island. The crew zoomed across the gangway onto the sand. Everyone was excited about the chance to hunt for treasure. But they were also excited to play in the waves and dig on the beach and romp through the trees. After weeks on a stinky pirate ship, it was time to run free!

As the rest of the puppies played fetch and chased waves, the oldest member of the pirate crew grumped and growled. Old Salt, a peg-legged Bernese mountain dog, had very strong opinions about treasure.

"What's wrong, Old Salt?" asked Wally. He dragged a nice, thick stick over for the old pirate

to chew on. "You don't look excited about our treasure hunt."

"Well, pup, I've always found that treasure hunts are more trouble than they're worth." He chewed the stick thoughtfully.

"What do you mean?" Wally asked.

"Sometimes pups forget to enjoy the treasure they already have," Old Salt said. Wally looked at him curiously, but the old dog would say nothing more.

Wally ran off to play with the pugs and Henry. The pugs had found some hollow bamboo shoots that were fun to blow air through. Soon, Piggly found a bush full of wild blueberries. After she ate her fill, she loaded her bamboo straw with berries and blew them at her friends. Some berries pinged off the dogs' fur, while others splatted on contact.

Henry lay down to rest on the warm beach sand. This gave Piggly and Puggly another excellent idea. They began to dig. In just a few minutes, Henry was totally covered in sand. That looked like fun to Wally, so he lay down next to Henry. The pugs buried him, too.

The four friends were having such a great time that they didn't realize the rest of the crew had gathered on the other end of the beach, by the edge of a dark green jungle. They were about to set off on the treasure hunt . . . without Wally, Henry, and the pugs!

"Wait for us!" Wally yelped, but the others were too far away to hear. He wriggled and squirmed in the sand, but it was no use. He was buried up to his neck.

Piggly and Puggly dug Wally and Henry out of the sand as fast as they could. But their legs were short, and it wasn't fast enough. By the time Wally and Henry were free, the rest of the crew was long gone.

Wally ran to the edge of the trees and sniffed

around for a familiar scent. But there were too many new and exciting smells. He couldn't figure out which ones belonged to his crew— or where they might have gone.

"It looks like we're on our own," said Henry, coming up behind Wally. He reached into his pocket, and Wally heard something crinkle. "But in case you were wondering? I still have the map!"

Treasure Talk

"We still have the map!" Wally cried joyfully. He leaped in the air. He rolled around in the sand. He wagged his tail as hard as he could. Then he realized something, and his tail stopped wagging. "But we're also all alone." He swallowed and pulled his golden velvety ears in close against his head. Wally hated to be alone.

He peered into the jungle. The trees were emerald green and massive. They were even higher than the crow's nest on the *Salty Bone*.

Until then, the ship was the tallest thing Wally had ever seen.

"We're not alone," said Puggly. "We have each other."

"And the map!" Piggly reminded them. "Let's figure out which way we're supposed to go." She snatched the map out of Henry's hand.

"Treasure!" screeched Puggly. Puggly *loved* beautiful things. She couldn't wait to see what jewels and riches Growlin' Grace might have buried. "Treasure, treasure, treasure, treasure—"

Piggly bumped her rump against her sister's to get her to stop yapping. They had work to do. Treasure-tracking work.

Wally unrolled the map and held it open with his two front paws. There were a lot of lines and symbols and squiggly stuff. None of it made sense.

Henry got down on his knees beside Wally.

"Look! Here is where we are—this beach. And there's the X. In case you were wondering, X always marks the treasure spot." He pointed at a big X in the bottom corner of the map.

Wally looked at the map. The path toward the X started at the beach and wove through the jungle. He knew they were running out of time. If they didn't chase after the captain and the others soon, they would be too far behind to ever catch up. And when the captain realized he didn't have the map? He would be furious. Wally did not like when the captain was angry.

"The others went this way," Wally said, nosing into the trees. "We can hunt for the crew and the treasure at the same time."

Because he was the tallest, Henry led. Wally followed, with Piggly and Puggly trotting along at the rear.

Wally was born on a farm and had only heard

about the jungle in stories. The real thing was much darker and deeper. Birdsong and monkey screeches echoed all around them. Strange, rich smells of flowers and bark and animals blasted them from all sides. Crooked branches scraped their fur and grabbed their tails. Soon the leaves were so thick they blocked out the sun. The deeper they went, the darker it got.

It got very, very dark.

"In case you were wondering, there are probably hundreds of different birds and animals watching us right this very minute," Henry said. "Snakes, too. They're very sneaky."

Sometimes Wally wished Henry didn't know quite so much.

Puggly stood taller and walked with her tail held high. She *loved* to be noticed. Wally, however, crept low to the ground.

Wally felt something ooze across his paw. He

yanked his paw up and shook the thing away. It was just a damp leaf. A moment later, he was sure a snake was crawling up his hind leg. But it was only a vine.

Giggling, Piggly wrapped her legs around the vine and swung herself off the ground. "Ahooooooooy!" she barked, whipping through the trees.

Puggly aimed her bamboo berry shooter at her sister as she swung by. "*Ptooey!*" she spat, blowing berries at Piggly. "Gotcha!"

Their barks echoed through the jungle. Wally wondered if anyone was listening.

The pugs swung back and forth on the vines until they got bored. "I'm starving!" Piggly whined, plopping back to the ground.

"And I'm ready to find the treasure," said Puggly. "I hope it's a box full of sparkly stuff. With a crown fit for a queen like me!"

Suddenly, Henry stopped. "Listen," he said.

The three dogs all parked on their haunches
and did as they were told. "I don't hear anything," murmured Wally.

"It's quiet," said Henry. "Too quiet." He
studied the map. He marked their place with

his finger. "If we were on the right track, we would hear the rest of the crew barking. What if we lost the trail?"

Wally and the pugs sniffed at the ground, trying to pick up their friends' scent. Wally thought he caught a whiff of Steak-Eye, who always smelled like stew.

He snuffled in the dirt, trying to sniff out the captain or Curly. But instead, he discovered a trace of someone he didn't recognize.

There was someone else nearby. Or some-*thing.*

He looked up to ask the pugs if they smelled it, too. And that's when he saw it: a pair of eyes, hiding in the darkness. Something was watching them. Something big! Wally pressed his body against Henry's legs to urge his friend to move. Then he barked to signal danger to the pugs.

Henry frowned into the darkness. Piggly and Puggly growled. Wally shivered.

The creature's eyes glowed in the dark.

That's when all four brave pirates had the same idea at the same time: *run!*

A Beastly Buzz

The four friends charged through the woods. They leaped over stumps and ducked under branches. They scrambled between bushes and wiggled over wet leaves and twisty vines. Wally wasn't sure where they were running to, and he wasn't sure what they were running away from. But he was sure it was something awful. And he was sure he was going to keep running until he couldn't run anymore.

Finally, when his lungs felt as if they might burst, Wally slowed and then stopped. The pugs were out of breath, too. Their tongues hung from their mouths like fat pieces of ham. Henry bent over to catch his breath and take a swig of water from his canteen.

"Did you see it?" Wally asked Piggly. "Did you see what was watching us?"

Piggly arfed. "Aye. It was a great and terrible beastie."

"A monster," Puggly panted. "Must be after the treasure."

"A monster?" Wally asked, wide-eyed. "What kind of monster?"

"Well, I didn't *exactly* see the thing," Piggly said. "But I know it was huge."

"Be glad it didn't catch us," Puggly agreed.

Wally was very glad. He was also very tired. He turned in a circle and lay down, panting.

Maybe he could sneak in a little nap. As soon as he closed his eyes, he heard it.

Buzz . . . Buzz . . . He opened one eye and saw the pugs batting around a papery grayish-brown ball. Except the ball was buzzing.

"Arr-*ooooo!*" Wally woofed. He knew that sound. That was the sound of angry bees. Piggly and Puggly were playing with a beehive!

A moment later, the bees swarmed. Wally felt a sharp sting on his nose. "Ouch!" he cried, swatting at his nose with a paw.

"In case you were wondering," Henry said, "there's more where that came from. We better get out of here fast!"

The group ran faster than ever, trying to escape the swarm of angry bees. Puggly's beads and ribbons kept catching on things in the jungle. More than once, Wally and Henry had to turn back to help untangle her. Piggly's wiggly

belly jiggled. She had a hard time keeping up. Finally, Henry tugged Piggly into his arms and carried her.

Just as Wally started to feel like he couldn't run any farther, they reached the edge of a river. *Perfect!* Wally thought. He was pretty sure bees couldn't swim. He splashed straight into the water. Henry followed. The pugs buried themselves in some mud on the riverbank.

The cool water was just shallow enough for Wally to stand with his head out of the water. Which was a lucky thing, because Wally didn't know how to swim.

Henry crouched low beside Wally. He held the map high in his hand, safe and dry above the water. "In case you were wondering, we lost the bees, mate."

They were no closer to finding the rest of the crew. But at least they were safe from stings. That was something to celebrate.

Wally splashed around, lapping eagerly at the water. Piggly and Puggly giggled as they played in the mud. They almost forgot about the bees and the treasure hunt and the—

"Beastie!" barked Wally, suddenly remembering. He could hear something crashing through the trees. There was no time to run.

Seconds later, the leaves parted. A black-and-white blur sped toward them at full speed, then stopped just before it hit the water. The creature's eyes glowed bright, the same way they had in the bushes. But now a long speckled nose, two floppy ears, and a panting tongue surrounded the glowing eyes. The monster they'd been running from was nothing more than a spotted Dalmatian puppy, no bigger than Wally.

"Greetings!" the spotted pup said, jumping into the water beside Wally. She swam around, then hopped out onto shore and shook herself off. "Thanks for that grand chase. And welcome to my island! Will you be staying long?"

Growlin' Grace's Adventures

Piggly and Puggly backed into the bushes. As lifelong pirates, they had been taught never to trust anything or anyone right away.

But Wally and Henry—who were still learning the pirate ropes—were friendlier. "Ahoy," said Wally, wagging his tail. "Do you live here?"

"Certainly," said the pup. There was a small black spot around one of her eyes that made it look like she was wearing an eye patch. "I've lived here all my life. The other dogs call me Rosie

because of the pink spot on my nose." Rosie
sniffed the air to show them her partly pink
patch.

"I'm Wally. This is my best mate, Henry.
And we're—"

"In case you were wondering," Henry inter-
rupted, "we're searching for Growlin' Grace's
greatest treasure."

"Of course," said Rosie. "Many pirates come

to our island searching for treasure. But none have ever found it."

"Do you know where it is?" Wally asked. A personal tour guide would be much more helpful than an old treasure map, any day!

Rosie laughed. "It's my job to protect the treasure, silly pup. Not lead people to it."

Wally's eyes widened. "So you're like a guard dog for Growlin' Grace?"

"Treasure Keeper." Rosie sat tall and proud. "Do you know the story of how Growlin' Grace's treasure came to live on this island?"

"No," said Wally. He lay down on the riverbank and waited for Rosie to tell the tale. Wally loved stories. "Piggly! Puggly! Do you want to hear a story?"

The two pugs poked their short snouts out of the bushes and eyed Rosie. Rosie let the little dogs approach her and sniff. After a couple of good long snorts, the pugs were satisfied that the danger had passed. They settled in on the cool grass of the riverbank and panted.

Rosie lowered her voice and began. "Many years ago, when the great salt waters were filled with giant beasts and terrible monsters, there lived a puppy pirate captain more brave and daring than any who had come before her. She and her crew were bold explorers who loved adventures. They sailed across the world, meeting many enemies and discovering new lands and waters along the way. Some people say Growlin' Grace had a touch of magic in her."

Piggly squirmed forward and asked, "Why?"

Rosie smiled. "Because everywhere Grace went, she found treasure."

"Jewels?" Puggly wondered.

"Gold?" said Wally.

Rosie cocked her head to one side. "No one

knows for sure. But Growlin' Grace became famous for her treasure-hunting skills. Every pirate from all corners of the world wanted to join her crew, so they could have a chance to be a part of Grace's explorations and discoveries. They say the adventures her crew had were the greatest in all the world. But one day . . ." Rosie stopped to lap up some water in the river.

Henry, who had been relaxing on his back on the bank, opened one eye and smiled at Rosie sleepily.

"One day what?" asked Wally. "What happened?"

"One day, her ship set off in search of the legendary Sea Slug. It was a beast so terrible no ship could pass it without being slimed or gobbled up. Before they set sail, Growlin' Grace decided she should leave her most precious treasure somewhere for safekeeping. So she came to the Boneyard. She buried her treasure here and surrounded it with the watchful eyes of my pack. She made just one map that would help her find the booty when she finally came back for it."

"Did they find the Sea Slug?" Wally whispered. "What happened then?"

Rosie's eyes sparkled. "Well . . ."

Piggly and Puggly snorted and spun in circles, eager to hear the rest of the story.

"Growlin' Grace and her crew sailed into the deepest, darkest uncharted waters . . . and were never heard from again."

Wally gasped. "Never again? She never came back for her treasure?"

"No one knows what happened to them," said Rosie. "Some pups are certain that Grace knew she would never be back. Many believe she left her treasure here with the hopes that

someday another worthy puppy pirate might find it. But no one has. And now her treasure map is long lost."

Wally leaped to his feet. He yipped, "No it's not! We have the map!"

Piggly and Puggly tried to shush him, but it was too late. Suddenly, dozens more spotted pups appeared at the edges of the trees. Rosie's tail straightened in warning. Her smile was gone when she said, "I hope you don't think you'll be taking that treasure. Many unworthy pups have tried before, but none have succeeded. As Treasure Keepers, it's our job to make sure it stays that way."

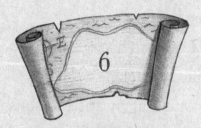

Trapped!

"What makes you think we be unworthy?" barked Piggly.

"What's *unworthy*?" whispered Wally.

Puggly said, "She's tryin' to say we don't deserve to find that treasure." Then she growled and blew berries through the bamboo straw, warning the other dogs to get back. "Yo ho haroo! We're gonna find that treasure, and there's nothing you can do to stop us."

Rosie bared her teeth. "Oh, we don't need to stop you. The booby traps will do that job for us."

"Booby traps?" Wally asked nervously.

Rosie chuckled, but there was nothing friendly about it. "This island is full of them," she said. "Growlin' Grace didn't want just anyone finding her treasure. So we made sure our traps would catch any unworthy pirates trying to get their paws on her booty. In fact, they've already caught the rest of your crew."

Wally yipped in alarm. "What do you mean?"

"See for yourself," Rosie said, cocking her head in the direction of the dark jungle.

"Come on!" Piggly said, charging off into the trees.

Puggly followed close behind. "We have to save our crew!" she barked.

Rosie glared at Wally and warned him, "The pack and I will be watching. I would wish you luck . . . but luck won't help you now." Without another word, she and her pack slipped back into the bushes and disappeared.

Wally and Henry raced into the jungle after the pugs. The four friends climbed over tree roots. They charged through the thick, damp vines. But everyone stopped when a familiar bark rang out ahead.

"Avast! That sounds like Curly!" shouted Wally. He took off toward the barking.

When Wally ran as fast as his fluffy legs would carry him, it was impossible for the pugs or Henry to match his pace. So Wally was the first to see what Curly was barking about . . . and it wasn't good.

The whole crew was trapped inside a giant net. The trap was hanging from a tall branch,

spinning round and round and round!

"Wally! You're alive!" yipped Curly as soon as she saw Wally flying toward her. She was the only puppy pirate who was not stuck in the net. "I'm so glad you found us. I can't get these scurvy dogs out of that trap on me own."

"What happened?" panted Wally.

Curly quickly said, "Well, we were following the captain through the forest, lookin' for the treasure. We made it this far across the island before Captain Red Beard told us he forgot the map on the ship. That's when we realized we had lost the four of you, too."

Piggly waddled into the clearing and collapsed in a heap at Curly's feet. Puggly rolled on top of her sister and snorted. Henry came last and announced, "Looks like you all are in a whole lot of trouble."

Curly sniffed. "We stopped to come up with a plan, and the captain was feelin' hungry. When he saw a big, meaty pile of bones, he pounced. But the bones were bait for a booby trap! We all got scooped up into the net." She boasted, "I'm tiny, so I was able to wriggle out. But the others are stuck, and I can't get 'em out on me own."

The net spun slowly, fifteen feet in the air. Inside, the crew was a tangle of snouts and paws.

"Ow! Watch yourself!" yelped Old Salt when Red Beard's tail thwacked him in the head.

The ship's cranky cook, Steak-Eye, howled, "Arrrrr-*ooooo!* Ya scurvy dog, you're squeezin' me into jelly." The tiny cook was squished between an enormous Great Dane and the captain, right in the middle of the pile of puppies.

Piggly giggled. "Look at Steak-Eye! His eyes might pop outta his head."

Puggly snorted. "His eyes *always* look like that. He's a Chihuahua."

Captain Red Beard rolled and spun again. "Why's it so crowded in this hammock? This might be the worst nap I've ever taken."

Old Salt groaned. "This is a trap, Captain, remember? Not a hammock. This is not a nap."

"This is a trap?" yelped Red Beard. "Oh, right. A trap." Suddenly, he began to howl, *"Help! Help!* We're trapped."

Curly sighed and looked at the others. "Anyone have an idea how to get them down?"

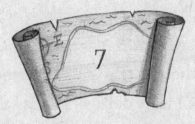

Knot So Fast

Wally, the pug sisters, and Curly discussed the best way to free the rest of the crew. "How 'bout I shoot 'em down?" suggested Puggly. She and Piggly blew berries at their friends, giggling merrily when they splatted against fur.

"Maybe the crew could chew themselves out of the rope?" suggested Wally.

Piggly barked in agreement. "Steak-Eye has super sharp teeth."

Curly thought for a moment. "What we really

need is for someone to untie the knot." She glanced at Henry, then said to Wally, "Your boy has hands. Maybe he can be of some use."

Wally thought this was a great idea, and it seemed like Henry did, too. He had already begun to climb a nearby tree. "In case you were wondering," Henry announced, "this is a simple poacher's knot. Every great pirate knows knots! All I need to do is untie it."

As Henry worked, Wally rushed to the edge of the clearing and gathered palm fronds in his mouth. He piled them under the trap. When his mates fell from the tree, he wanted to make sure they had something soft to land on.

Henry used the hard edges of the magnet to loosen the tricky parts of the knot that his fingers couldn't grasp. The trapped puppy pirates yelped as the trap began to swing to and fro. With each one of Henry's tugs, the pouch full of dogs swayed faster and faster.

"My tummy feels worse than when Steak-Eye makes mystery meat hash," one dog moaned.

The knot began to slip. Then—

Snap!

The net broke open. The crew of puppy pirates rained down onto the leafy jungle floor. The dogs yelped and squealed when they

landed, but no one seemed badly hurt.

Wally ran over to check on Old Salt. The old dog was licking a scrape on his paw, but otherwise seemed fine. "Are you okay, Old Salt?" asked Wally.

Old Salt muttered, "Don't be worryin' about me. I've survived much worse things than a little fall from a tree."

After the crew had all licked their wounds, Wally told the others about meeting Rosie and her pack.

Captain Red Beard said, "Treasure Keepers, eh? And they said there are more traps? Ah, I do love a good booby trap. When ya find a trap, it means you're on the right track! It means there's somethin' ahead that's worth protecting."

"We may well be on the right track," snipped Curly, "but without the map, we're no closer to finding the treasure now than we were a year ago."

"We have the map," announced Wally. "Henry remembered to bring it along when we left the ship."

Curly looked surprised. "Your boy? The human? *He* has the map?"

"Yep," said Wally proudly. He nudged the map out of his friend's pocket with his nose.

Curly cocked her head at Henry again. "Well, shiver me timbers, the boy's done two things right in one day."

Henry unrolled the map. Then, together, he and Red Beard studied it. "All right, me crew," said Red Beard, taking charge. "Carry on this way! We be looking for an X to mark the spot."

Curly said, "Um, Captain? I don't think there's an actual X by the treasure. Usually, the X just marks the spot on the map."

Red Beard looked confused, then nodded. "Ah, yes. Of course. That's what I meant. Okay. Onward!"

Before they set off, Steak-Eye passed around snacks. Soon, everyone but Piggly— who was *always* hungry—had a full belly and was ready to continue.

Then Curly suggested that each of the dogs find a giant leaf to use as protection from the hot sun. They found a tree with leaves shaped like curved umbrellas. When they were strapped to the puppy pirates' backs with vines, the leaves

helped keep them cool and comfortable in the midday heat.

As they tiptoed over a fraying rope bridge, Red Beard kept them all calm by singing pirate songs about treasure.

While they walked single file along the ridge of a steep mountain, Old Salt helped them focus by telling stories from his many years of pirate adventures.

And when they snuck under a roaring waterfall—protected from the spray by their leafy umbrellas—Piggly and Puggly told jokes to keep everyone smiling. It felt good to have the whole crew back together.

Just past the waterfall, the captain ordered his crew to stop. "Avast!" Up ahead, something shiny glinted in the sunlight. Everyone squinted for a better look. Red Beard's tail began to wag, and he barked, "The booty!"

They all ran. For there it was, right in the open for anyone to see: *a golden treasure chest*!

Henry and Wally whooped with joy as they chased after the others. But when they neared the chest, Wally realized something wasn't right. On the map, the X to mark the spot was in the middle of a big, open space, near the ocean. But this treasure chest was sitting at the top of a huge hill. Here, they were surrounded by trees and rocks and the waterfall.

"Don't act without thinking," Old Salt warned them. "Too many pups lose their heads at the sight of treasure."

But the captain was already nosing open the lid of the treasure box. When it popped open, a horrible smell came rushing out at the crew. It was worse than rotten apples and spoiled meat. The dogs all scrambled backward, but they soon realized that the smell was the least of their problems.

Something rumbled, and the ground began to shake. Rocks danced around them as the earth tilted like their ship did in a terrible storm. The sand and dirt under their feet slipped away, taking Red Beard and his crew along for a ride.

"It's a mudslide!" woofed the captain. "What do we do?"

Thinking quickly, Piggly and Puggly came up with an idea.

"Everyone untie your shade leaf!" Piggly

said. "You can use it as a surfboard to surf the mud."

"Like this!" Puggly cried, leaping onto her leaf and riding a wave of mud all the way to the bottom of the hill.

Piggly threw herself down after her sister, howling with glee. "Yo ho haroooo!"

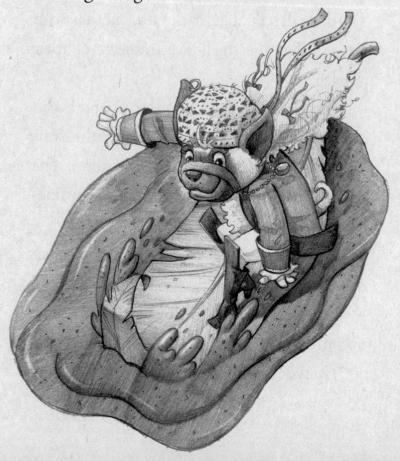

The other dogs leaped onto their leaves and followed them down.

"Aye, aye!" barked Red Beard. "I'm surfin'!"

Right at the bottom of the hill, next to a gorgeous sand beach, was the biggest mudhole any of them had ever seen. *Splat!* The sticky mud felt cold and refreshing after a long day of treasure hunting.

Puggly barked, "This is pug-glorious!"

Wally agreed. He wished *all* booby traps were this fun. He and the other pups wrestled and rolled and dug holes in the mud for a few moments before they heard Old Salt's warning bark.

The ground rumbled again. "It's another trap!" Wally yelped. "Quick, we have to get out of here!" But it was too late. No one was going anywhere.

A Little Riddle

Dozens of wooden poles sprouted out of the dirt. They stretched up, up, up toward the clouds. The puppy pirate crew scrambled to get out of the mud, but the gooey ground made it impossible for them to move quickly enough.

The poles were too close together to squeeze through. Too sturdy to push over. Too thick to chew through.

There was no way out.

"Sticks!" howled Captain Red Beard joyfully. "Lots of sticks for us to chew!"

"Not sticks," mumbled Old Salt. "This is a cage. We're trapped."

Wally paced the edges of the cage. He noticed something strange. Each bar had a number carved into it. The numbers went in order, from 1 to 317. A cage with more than *three hundred*

bars? Wally sighed. It was hopeless. Even Curly couldn't escape this trap.

Henry pulled out the map. "I don't see a cage on this map anywhere, so this must be another booby trap to guard the treasure."

"Thank you, Captain Obvious," grumbled Curly.

Wally tugged at the first mate's tail, warning her to leave his friend alone.

"Look!" sniffed Piggly. She, too, had been sniffing around the edges of the large cage, searching for hidden food. Instead, she found strange words carved into one of the bars:

IF YE BE WORTHY, THEN YE SHALL
KNOW ... THAT THREE BY THREE IS HOW
YE SHALL GO.

"I wonder if it could be a clue?" asked Wally. "There are numbers in the riddle and numbers carved into the poles. That must mean *something*."

"I bet these words are a clue!" agreed Henry.

"Three and three . . . ," muttered Red Beard. "I've got . . . let's see . . . one, two, three paws. Three paws!"

"Four paws," corrected Old Salt with a sigh. "I've got three paws."

Red Beard went on. "Dogs have one nose. Two eyes. Three what?"

"Hmm, three by three . . . ," said Curly. "What if it's simple math? Three plus three is

six. What happens if we press the pole with a six carved into it?"

Piggly launched herself at the bar labeled with the number six. As soon as she hit it, it swung open and she found herself on the other side of the cage. "Ahoy in there!" she snorted at her friends.

Puggly tried next, but this time, the sixth bar wouldn't budge. She barked in confusion. "What now?"

The puppies didn't get it. They had solved the riddle. So why did it only work once? And how were the rest of them supposed to get out?

"Three by three," Wally murmured, knocking ideas around in his head. Suddenly, he came up with a new one. "What if we have to go *another* three?" he said.

"Keep up, Walty," the captain snapped. "We can't *go* anywhere. That's the problem."

"No, what if we *count* another three?" Wally

asked. "We started with the sixth bar. What's three past that?"

Puggly counted it out with her paws. "Seven . . . eight . . . nine!" She flung herself at the ninth bar—and sailed right through.

"In case you were wondering, I think we need to count by threes until we're all out of here!" Henry said.

Old Salt went next, counting three more bars to number twelve, and pushing through to freedom. Then Steak-Eye (fifteen), then Wally (eighteen), then the rest of the crew. Like a good captain, Red Beard took up the rear—but Wally had to tell him which bar to press. Hard as he tried, Red Beard couldn't seem to count by threes.

On the other side of the cage, tall palm trees grew out of the sand. Wally thought they looked like little rockets exploding high above the beach.

When Henry took out the treasure map to check their location, Wally noticed that Rosie and the pack of Dalmatians were back. They were waiting right along the water's edge. Wally had a feeling that that meant the treasure was close by.

Wally introduced the captain and his crew to the Treasure Keepers.

Rosie growled, "Somehow, you escaped the net trap. Then you found a way to *enjoy* the mudslide. You have solved Growlin' Grace's riddle. I will admit that your band of pirates has gotten much closer to the treasure than any others who have come before you." The Dalmatian stood tall. "The map has taken you this far, but now you're on your own."

Red Beard gazed around with his sharp terrier eyes. "On the map, there's an X by a tree. So there must be treasure under one of these trees."

Wally thought that sounded right. There was just one problem: *Which tree?* He started sniffing around in the sand. If he couldn't see the treasure, maybe he could *smell* it.

"We're dogs," Curly reminded her crew. "We were built to dig. We know the treasure's under here somewhere. So I say we dig!"

The puppy pirates took off. Sand and paws flew everywhere. Rosie and the Treasure Keepers watched carefully. As the afternoon stretched on, they began to smile. Not one of the puppy pirates had any luck. Soon the entire beach was filled with holes—but there was still no sign of treasure.

Wally stopped for a break. He was hot, sandy, and thirsty. Around him, he could see that the rest of the crew was growing tired, too. Piggly had settled in under a tree, where she was trying to knock open a coconut with her magnet. Puggly was grooming herself, trying to clean the mud off her ribbons. Henry, who had no paws, was still struggling to dig his first hole.

What if this doesn't work? Wally wondered. What if they *never* found Growlin' Grace's treasure? He knew they must be missing an important clue. Growlin' Grace wanted to make her treasure hard to find. But she wouldn't have made it *impossible*. He stared up into the vast blue sky, watching the trees flutter in the ocean air. And that's when he saw it—an X! Not an X on the ground, but an X made of trees.

Two palm trees tilted out of the sand. Their trunks crossed each other. Reaching high into the air, side by side, they looked very much like an X.

What a clever way to mark the spot!

Wally leaped up and began to bark. "The trees!" he yipped. "The X is *in* the trees!"

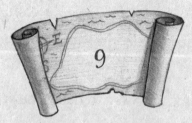

Trick Sand

The puppy pirates all gathered under the giant X. They let Captain Red Beard dig first. He picked a spot right between the two trees and pawed at the wet sand.

"Arrrr!" growled Red Beard. "Look out, treasure, here I come!"

Then he began to sink.

Down, down, down.

"It's quicksand!" yowled Curly.

"Quicksand? You're kiddin' me." Red Beard's four paws were sinking quickly in the oozing muck.

Four dogs on the crew stepped forward to help save their captain. One pulled at Red Beard's ear with his teeth. Another snapped the captain's beard in her mouth and tugged. A third got a mouthful of the scruff at the back of Red Beard's neck. Finally, the big Great Dane

got his nose up under the captain's belly and lifted. Working together, they dragged Red Beard to safety.

Growlin' Grace's treasure was down at the bottom of that quicksand. The puppy pirates were sure of it. They were close enough that they could almost *smell* it! But what good did it do? They couldn't dig without sinking. And if they couldn't dig, how could they get their paws on the treasure?

"We've got ourselves a little sit-you-station," said Red Beard, rubbing his paws in dry sand to clean off the quicksand.

"I think you mean *situation*, Captain?" offered Piggly.

"As I said," growled Red Beard. "This is a situation with no pollution."

"*Solution?*" wondered Curly.

"Exactly!" agreed Red Beard. "So what is it?"

"The solution?" said Curly. "Well, the only solution I can think of is for one brave and mighty pirate to take the plunge. One of us has to get down there."

"I already did that," said Red Beard. "It made my toes feel funny."

"I've got an idea." A shaggy Old English sheepdog giggled. "Let's dangle one of the pugs from a leash and drop 'em in. We've got two on our crew, so we can afford to lose one, eh?"

Piggly and Puggly growled and snapped at the sheepdog.

Curly stood as tall as a tiny poodle could get. "I'll go in. I'm small and light, and I can hold my breath longer than any other dog on the crew. If you tie a rope around me, you should be able to pull me out once I have the treasure."

"No," Wally yelped. "It's too risky!" Being on the crew meant looking out for his fellow pirates.

He couldn't let Curly put herself in danger.

"You got a better idea, pup?" Curly asked. "Because otherwise—"

"Wait!" Wally said. "I do have a better idea. It's ... it's ..." He thought very hard. Then Wally snatched Piggly's magnet out of her paws. He remembered the pugs dangling the magnet through the spy hole that morning, and how they told him it would stick to the metal map box. If the treasure chest had metal on it, maybe the magnet could pull it to the surface. "We can use this!"

Captain Red Beard was impressed. "It's worth a shot."

Using his expert knot skills, Henry tied the magnet to the end of Piggly's bamboo shooter with vines. It was like a fishing rod—with a giant magnet dangling from the end.

Captain Red Beard held the rod as the crew

lowered the rope into the quicksand. At first, the magnet just sat like a lump on the top of the sand. But after a few moments, it began to sink into the pit. Slowly at first, then faster. The line stretched and pulled. The pups held their breath as they waited for it to hit something. The magnet just kept sinking—deeper and deeper and deeper.

Red Beard worked with the strongest pups on the crew to hold the pole tight. But it seemed that the sand was stronger. Before long, the line grew tight. And the sand began to tug the dogs toward the quicksand.

They had almost run out of rope. If the magnet didn't hit the chest soon, this treasure hunt would be a bust.

Snap!

Everyone felt it when the magnet snapped on to something deep in the ground. When the team of pups pulled on the rope with their teeth, they felt sure *something* was on their line. They pulled and pulled and pulled and pulled and—

Pop! The treasure chest came flying out of the quicksand. The crew dragged it onto solid ground. Everyone gathered around, even Rosie and her pack.

"Oh, my!" gasped Rosie. "It's Growlin' Grace's treasure chest. You found it!"

Even though the chest was coated in gooey sand, it was easy to see the huge jewels gleaming on the top of chest. Puggly squealed, eager to pop it open. "Jewels! Jewels! Jewels!" she said, bubbling with excitement.

Captain Red Beard urged everyone to step back. "Give the treasure room to breathe," he said. Then he eased open the latch and flipped the lid. The puppies rushed forward again. No one could wait to see what was inside.

When Wally poked his nose up over the edge of the chest, his hopes—and everyone else's—came crashing down. For inside the chest was . . . a bunch of old maps.

The captain scratched his beard and said what everyone was thinking. "Is that all?"

The Real Treasure

Wally had never seen a real pirate treasure before. But he was pretty sure there was supposed to be a lot more gold.

"I was hoping for at least a few yummy dog treats," muttered Piggly.

"Just maps," said Henry glumly. "This was a whole lot of hassle for a bunch of old maps."

"At least they aren't blank!" Puggly said.

Wally caught Rosie looking at the rest of her pack. She seemed as surprised as everyone else!

Curious, Wally nosed around inside the box. One of the pieces of parchment was different from all the others. It was a letter. Carefully, he pulled it out with his teeth.

"What's this?" asked Henry, taking it gently from Wally's mouth. "Ooh! It's a letter from Growlin' Grace."

To the worthy pirates who have found me bounty:

Congratulations. You have found my greatest treasure.

Bet you thought you'd find gold, eh? Ha!

Sure, I found plenty of riches in me travels. But in all me years as a pirate, I learned that the best treasure any pirate can hope for is the promise of more adventure.

In this box, you will find the maps me crew put together of all our greatest travels. These maps will lead you to the strangest and most wondrous places I've seen in all me days. I'm leaving them for a new group of worthy pirates. I hope you will use them to guide and inspire your own adventures.

Have fun. Make sure you add to me collection with new travels of your own.

Ahoy, mighty pirates!

—Growlin' Grace

When they had finished reading the letter, everyone sat quietly. Finally, Captain Red Beard broke the silence and cheered, "Hip, hip hooray!"

The rest of the crew joined in and cheered, too. More adventures! This *was* the greatest treasure Growlin' Grace could have left them. More than riches or jewels or the yummiest bones in all the world.

Only Puggly looked disappointed. She had really been hoping for a crown.

Wally nudged his friend and said, "Don't be sad, Puggly. Now that we have all these maps, we're sure to find a crown fit for a queen on one of our *next* adventures. Anyway, you're the fanciest pirate on our crew, even without jewels."

That cheered her up. She pranced around the beach.

"Let's get this treasure chest back to the ship," said Red Beard. "Adventure awaits!"

"Wait," said Rosie, stepping forward. "You can't take our treasure!"

"You said you wouldn't stop us from searching for the treasure," Wally reminded Rosie.

"Exactly," Rosie said. "We didn't stop you. And you found it. Now you can go."

"We're not leaving without that treasure!" Red Beard barked.

"And you're not leaving *with* it." Rosie and her pack stepped between the pirate crew and the treasure chest. The two packs stared each other down.

Old Salt coughed and said, "I can see you Dalmatians want to keep the treasure here."

"If you take the treasure," yapped Rosie, "then the Boneyard is just a plain old island! No one will come here to search for treasure anymore. We won't have anything to protect!"

"But I know our captain would like to take

Growlin' Grace's maps to guide our crew's adventures," Old Salt continued.

Red Beard barked, "Finders keepers!"

"I have a solution," Old Salt said calmly. "Rosie, your pack doesn't actually want *this* treasure for yourselves . . . ya just want *some* treasure buried on the island. Is that true?"

Rosie nodded.

Old Salt coughed. "Then I think we owe it to these pups to bury a treasure on this island for another band of pirates to find someday. A great pirate should always leave a little something behind for safekeeping before heading off on the next adventure. Don'tcha think, Cap'n?"

Curly added, "Just think . . . hundreds of pirates could come to this island searching for *your* treasure, Captain Red Beard."

Red Beard's eyes lit up. "The Boneyard will be the hiding place for *Red Beard's* greatest treasure! I like the sound of that!"

Rosie and the other Dalmatians barked their approval.

The only trouble was, no one had any idea what they could bury. They had no gold, or maps, or jewels.

Finally, Wally had an idea. "What if we each bury something that's special to us? Growlin' Grace's greatest treasure was her map collection, because they reminded her of her greatest adventures with her crew." He thought for a moment before he said, "My greatest treasure is my pirate bandanna. Because the day I got this bandanna, I knew I'd finally found my home on the ship with all of you."

"I'm gonna bury my best soup bone," said Steak-Eye, stepping forward to drop his bone into the box.

Puggly stepped forward, too. "And I'm going to bury my favorite necklace. That way, this box will have something *fancy* for the next gal who digs it up."

Piggly shot one last blueberry out of her bamboo shooter and said, "I'll hide this for another lucky prankster to find someday!"

Henry stepped forward and placed a picture he had drawn of him and Wally into the chest. Wally tossed his bandanna on top of it.

One by one, everyone on the crew dropped an item that meant something special to them into the chest. Soon it was filled to the top.

As Red Beard, the pugs, Wally, Henry, and the others lowered the chest back into the pit of quicksand, Rosie said, "Thank you. We promise to keep your greatest treasures safe for many years to come. And we hope you'll be back someday to fetch them."

"We will," promised Wally. "But not for a long time."

After all, now that they had Growlin' Grace's maps, they could go anywhere! Do anything!

As the Dalmatian puppies led the way down the beach, the *Salty Bone* loomed tall and proud in the distance. Wally couldn't wait to get back to the ship and set sail. Their next puppy pirate adventure was waiting!

Catnapped!

The kitten pirates
are on the prowl. . . .

Erin Soderberg

For sweet, smart, silly Ruby
—E.S.

CONTENTS

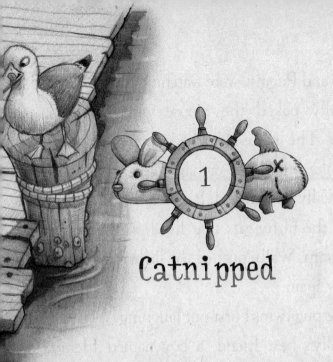

Catnipped

Wally's tail wagged at the sight of a soft, sweet mouse. His nose twitched. The gentle golden retriever slowed to a walk. He crept quietly over the wooden planks of the fishing pier. Closer . . . closer . . .

He pounced. "Gotcha!"

The mouse darted out of his grasp. Wally leaped on it again. This time, he caught it! The little critter stayed very, very still. Wally patted it with his paw and looked up. His two pug friends,

Piggly and Puggly, were watching him closely.

Wally poked the mouse with his nose. *Squeak!* The mouse smelled funny. It didn't smell like fur or dirt or hay, like all the other mice Wally had chased. It also didn't smell like one of the filthy rats that lived on the puppy pirate ship. Wally pushed the little mouse with his paw again.

The pug twins burst out laughing.

Wally's best friend, a boy named Henry, leaned toward Wally. "In case you were wondering, mate? That's a fake mouse. I think the pugs are playing pranks again."

"Aw, Wally," said Piggly. Her gold tooth glimmered in the early-morning sun. "We didn't mean to trick you."

Puggly wagged her tail. It was the puppy pirates' big day out in town, and the fancy pug was dressed in her favorite outfit—purple booties, a black velvet cap with a tall feather, and a fine golden cape. She sat primly and explained, "We're practicing our prank for the kitten pirates."

"This one is a classic," Piggly snorted. "We call it Catnipped Kitty. Have you ever seen a kitty with a nose full of catnip, mates?" She winked at the small group of puppy pirates who had gathered around.

Wally shook his head. He didn't know much about cats. He knew they hated water, had sharp claws, and were very stuck-up. (That's what the pugs had told him, anyway.) He also knew that the kitten pirates were the puppy pirates' worst enemies.

A bulldog named Spike whined, "Kitten pirates? Where?" The nervous bulldog looked like one of the toughest dogs on the puppy pirate crew. He could out-tug anyone if he wanted to. But he never did. Spike was a scaredy-dog.

"Look over there," Piggly said. She cocked her head in the direction of a pirate ship anchored far out in the harbor. "There's the kitten ship. It's called the *Nine Lives*."

The puppy pirate ship—the *Salty Bone*—was docked in town for the day. The puppy pirates needed to load up with supplies. The crew had a few hours off to run and play and explore before they set sail again.

Puggly winked. "That boatful of no-fun furballs is gonna be hanging out in town today, too. Which makes this the *purr*-fect day for pranks!"

A warning growl came from behind Wally. It was Old Salt, the oldest and wisest member of the puppy pirate crew. "Remember," the peg-legged Bernese mountain dog said, "we have a truce with the kitten pirates when we both sail into town. They leave us alone, and we leave them alone. Don't go lookin' for trouble."

The younger pups nodded.

"We don't need any of your monkey business," Old Salt said.

"No monkey business," Piggly promised.

As soon as Old Salt hobbled away, Puggly snorted, "Aye. Just a little kitty business."

"Here come the kitten pirates," Henry said, pointing.

A pair of blue-eyed Siamese kittens pranced toward them, tails held high.

"Here, kitty, kitty!" Piggly giggled. "I said, *heeeere*, kitty, kitties." She nudged her twin sister.

Puggly trotted down the fishing pier, swishing her curly tail back and forth. Now Wally saw that a piece of string was tied to Puggly's tail. The small stuffed mouse was at the end of the string. When Puggly wagged her tail, the little mouse bumped and thumped along after her. It looked and sounded just like a real mouse wiggling down the pier.

Swish!

Squeak!

Wiggle!

Piggly was laughing so hard she began to sneeze.

The two Siamese kittens hissed, "Ahoy, ya scurrrrvy dogs."

The pups growled back.

"Remember what Old Salt said," Wally whispered nervously. "We don't want any trouble."

"Trouble?" squeaked Spike. The fat bulldog dashed behind Wally. "Nope. We don't need trouble. No, sirree."

Piggly snorted, "Eh, they're just cats. How much trouble could a few furry felines be?"

Puggly wagged her tail harder. The stuffed

mouse flopped and squeaked on the wooden dock. Suddenly, the cats spotted it.

"Just wait, Wally," Piggly said, nudging him. "Watch and learn."

Wally hid his nose between his paws and peeked up at the kittens.

The kitten pirates crept toward the mouse. Their noses twitched. They arched their backs, popped their claws, and leaped.

Pounce!

Scaredy-Dogs

The Siamese kittens dove on the mouse. They chewed and tugged at the soft toy, pulling it off its string. They rubbed and rolled against it, then batted it into the air. They squealed and squeaked and flopped all over the wooden dock. They were totally out of control!

Wally had never seen anything like it before.

Piggly and Puggly roared with laughter. "There's catnip in the mice," Puggly explained.

"The stuff makes cats crazy. Even the boring ones."

The other puppy pirates crowded around to watch the kittens going wild. Even Spike crept close enough to see what was going on.

Both kittens screeched when they knocked over a bucket. The bucket tipped. Water flew

everywhere. Dozens of lobsters skittered out
and down the pier. Spike yelped and hid behind
Henry. But the cats ignored the lobsters' clack-
ing claws. They were too busy fighting over the
stuffed mouse.

Wally knew cats hated water, but these cats
barely seemed to notice that they were wet.

They bounced and tumbled in the puddle, then chased the toy farther down the dock. Their fur was soaked and matted with dirt.

"Will the catnip hurt them?" Wally asked Puggly.

"Nah," said Puggly. "Makes cats act funny. But once we take away the mice, they will be back to normal. Just embarrassed, is all."

The kittens' tongues lolled out of their mouths. As they wrestled, they rolled closer and closer to the edge of the pier. *What if they fall off?* Wally shuddered at the thought. *What if that was me? What if I was wearing the kittens' claws?* The ocean was cold and deep and wet. Wally would want someone to help him.

And he definitely wouldn't want to look so silly in front of all these other pirates.

"In case you were wondering?" Henry said, his eyebrows shooting up. "Cats are proud animals. They hate to be embarrassed like this."

Spike whispered, "I wish someone would take the mouse away from them."

Wally agreed with Henry and Spike. The pugs' prank had lasted long enough. If Old Salt were there, he would put an end to it.

But Old Salt wasn't there. Which meant someone else had to do it.

"Avast!" Wally said suddenly, surprising even himself.

"Eh?" barked Piggly.

Wally leaped onto the mouse. He ripped it out of the cats' claws and tossed the mouse toward the water. The kittens chased after it but stopped when the toy plopped into the ocean far below. Exhausted, both Siamese kittens collapsed onto the dock. Within seconds, they were fast asleep.

Wally tucked his tail between his legs. He could feel the pugs staring at him. Were they mad he had ruined their prank?

"Takes a mighty brave pirate to stick up for a cat," Puggly said finally. She didn't seem angry at all. She waddled down the pier, and a few paces away, she turned back to Wally. "You coming, Wally? We best be getting to the dog park to meet the rest of the crew."

"Aye!" Wally barked happily.

As he strutted through the crowds with Henry, Spike, Piggly, and Puggly, Wally could feel the town dogs' eyes on him and his mates. He walked tall and proud, showing off his pirate bandanna.

They passed through the market, gazing at all the carts and tables heaped with food. Steak-Eye, the ship's cook, was in a back alley arguing with a pup outside the butcher shop. As the feisty Chihuahua shouted and stomped, his tail whacked to and fro. Bones and a basket of dog treats toppled to the ground. "No, I will *not* take scraps!" Steak-Eye yipped. "Top-choice meat only. I buy the best for me crew."

The butcher pup looked nervous. He offered a piece of crispy bacon to Steak-Eye to apologize. Wally laughed. Steak-Eye seemed scary, but the ship's cook was all bark and no bite.

Just past the market, Wally spotted the ship's first mate. "Curly!" The tough miniature poodle was slinking along the edge of a pink building. It looked like she was trying to hide. "Curly!" he shouted again. "The dog park is this way."

Curly ignored him and ducked inside the shop.

"Pampered Pooch?" Henry said, reading the sign on the door. He wrinkled his nose. "Why is she going in there?"

"Curly gets a trim and a perm every time we get shore leave. You think hair like that just does itself?" Puggly sniffed. "Me? I wake up like this. I'm what's called a natural beauty."

At the edge of the shops, the friends came to a large dog park. In the center of the park was a small clear pond. Many of the puppy pirates were splashing around in the deep water. It was hard to swim in the ocean because of the waves. But here on land, the dogs loved to swim and play.

All except Wally.

"Come on in, Walty!" Captain Red Beard barked.

Henry tossed a ball into the pond for Wally. But Wally didn't move. "What's wrong, mate?" Henry asked.

Wally didn't answer. This was the moment he had been dreading since he first joined the pirate crew. After all, what kind of puppy pirate is afraid to swim?

Back when he had been a bitty pup, Wally had fallen into a lake near the farm. When he

yelped for help, he got a mouthful of water and panicked. Somehow he had managed to pad-dle to shore. But as soon as Wally's paws had touched land, he began to shake with fear.

He had never tried to swim again. He was afraid.

Spike was chewing a stick nearby. He lifted his meaty head and whispered to Wally, "Scared of water, are ya? I get it, mate. There's nothing scarier than swimming. Except cats . . . and chickens . . . and bilge rats . . . and Steak-Eye . . . and grass that touches my belly . . . and those little snails that sometimes get stuck to the side of our ship . . . and . . ."

Wally didn't want to be a scaredy-dog like Spike. But he didn't want to tell a fib, either. So instead of explaining why he wasn't swimming, he stretched out against Henry's leg and took a nap.

Before long, the puppy pirate crew was joined by a group of town dogs eager to hear stories of pirate adventures. Everyone climbed out of the pond and shook off. The town dogs curled up in a pile, listening as Captain Red Beard told tall tales of life on the high seas.

"And then there was the time we found a

gazillion gold coins and *then* fought off six hundred cats plus the Sea Slug, all in one afternoon!"

"Not all in one day?" gasped a Labrador retriever.

"Absolushy!" Red Beard boasted, holding up a paw. "That means *yep* in . . . um, Piratish. Piratish language. We pirates speak a bazillion languages, y'know."

The rest of the puppy pirates snickered. Captain Red Beard had a habit of stretching the truth and making up words. The scraggly terrier captain gave his crew a look that said, *Quiet!* The puppy pirates all stopped laughing at once. But in the silence that followed, something else began to laugh.

Many somethings.

The dogs looked around. Where was the sound coming from?

Spike was the first to howl. "Kitten pirates! Everybody run!"

Cat-Attack

It was an ambush! The entire kitten crew was crawling over the hillside. The cats were clearly angry, all hisses and claws. The town pups ran off, but the puppy pirates prepared for a fight.

Most of the puppy pirates, anyway. Not Spike. He just roamed in circles, shaking with terror. "What do we do? What do we *do-oooo-ooooo*?"

Captain Red Beard pushed to the front of

his crew. He went nose to nose with the kitten captain. "We had a deal, Captain Lucinda the Loud! We no attacky you, you no attacky us."

Lucinda the Loud hissed. "We *had* a deal . . . until your pugs broke the rules. Bad dogs! You should know better than to play catnip pranks on Moopsy and Boopsy."

"Uh-oh," Piggly squeaked. She and Puggly quickly backed away from the face-off. They ducked beneath a leafy bush.

"Moopsy and Boopsy?" Puggly snorted, once they were safely out of sight. She tried to hide her giggles inside her cape. "The Siamese cats are named *Moopsy* and *Boopsy*?" Laughing and sneezing, she poked her sister. "Piggly, come with me. I've got an idea!"

No one but Wally noticed the pugs sneak away. All eyes were on the two pirate captains.

"You're outnumbered!" Lucinda the Loud

yelled. "You have no choice but to surrender."

"Never!" Red Beard barked. "Puppy pirates, prepare for battle!"

Lucinda the Loud was right: the puppies *were* outnumbered. They were also tired from a morning of playing in the pond. They had no energy left for a fight. But they had no other choice.

Hissssss!

Cats and dogs jumped at the strange sound. Little black spigots poked out of the grass all over the dog park. Then water came shooting out!

"Me fur!" Lucinda the Loud shrieked, trying to shield herself. The kitten pirates panicked and ran toward the trees for cover.

"En garde!" Puggly said, whipping her cape in the air. "Pugs to the rescue!"

Piggly cheered. "The best part of this park is a sprinkler system for hot days—and for cat attack-ack-ack-acks!"

Red Beard howled. The rest of the crew
joined in. "Flee, kitty cats, flee!" he barked joyfully. Even Lucinda the Loud was cowering
under a leafy tree. "Neener-nanner-noo-noo!"
Red Beard teased. "The puppy pirates win
again! Now, pups, to the ship. With paste!"

Curly said, "I think you mean *haste*, Captain Red Beard? Move fast, yes?"

"As I said: to the ship, with pasty haste!" The captain raced through the park, with the rest of the crew hot on his tail. The sprinklers couldn't stay on forever.

Wally stopped when he realized Spike wasn't with them. The bulldog was frozen in place near the pond, staring at a tiny kitten. She was perched on a branch, giving him the stink eye. "C'mon, Spike," Wally said, tugging his collar. "We need to get out of here before the sprinklers shut off."

Nearby, Piggly and Puggly were helping Steak-Eye and Old Salt drag the cook's big bag of steaks. The pugs urged the other two to go on ahead. "It's me and Puggly's fault we're in this mess," Piggly said. "We can get Henry to help us carry the steaks."

Steak-Eye squinted his bulgy eyes. "Fine. But

don't go stealin' me food, Piggly. I know *exactly* how many steaks the butcher put in that bag."

"Yeah, yeah," grumbled Piggly. Old Salt and Steak-Eye ran ahead. Piggly, Puggly, and Henry tugged at the bag of meat.

Wally and Spike caught up to them. Wally was trying to keep the scared bulldog calm. "Deep breaths, Spike. Let your tongue flap out. There you go."

Between the weight of the steaks and Spike's slow, shaky legs, the group of five soon fell far behind the rest of the crew. The cats glared at them from hiding spots in the trees. The water kept raining down.

"Do you hear something?" Piggly said, stopping abruptly. The others froze beside her.

"Something? What something?" Spike curled into a tight ball.

Then Wally heard it, too. A faint *woof* coming from above.

"Is there a *dog* in that tree?" Wally asked, confused. How could a pup climb a tree?

"Woof, woof, help me!" came a tiny voice from way up in the branches.

Henry, Wally, Puggly, and even Spike all rushed toward the tree. Only Piggly stayed where she was. "Is it just me, or does that sound a lot like—"

Plop! A net fell from the tree, right on top of Wally, Henry, Spike, and Puggly.

"—like a cat," Piggly finished.

Moopsy and Boopsy, the two Siamese cats, poked their heads out of the leafy branches high above the pups. "Ha-*ha*!" the two cats cheered together. "Now who's laughing, pugs?"

"You missed *me*, hair balls," Piggly taunted.

Wally barked, "Piggly, go for help! Run while you can."

Spike wailed, "Tell the others we've— we've—we've been *catnapped*!"

The Brig Jig

Wally, Henry, Puggly, and Spike were prisoners on the kitten ship.

"In case you were wondering, mates?" Henry said. He sat on the floor with his back against a cold, damp wall. Gently, he twisted the soft fur under Wally's chin. "This is not looking so good."

"Not looking good," Spike whimpered, closing his eyes. "Not looking good, not looking good, not looking—"

"Calm down, will you?" Puggly said primly. "So we're prisoners on the kitten ship. What's the big deal?"

"What's the big deal?" Spike howled. "They're *cats*!"

Moopsy and Boopsy had waited until the park sprinklers turned off. Then they leashed up their prisoners—even Henry—and led them out of the park. They were all long gone before Piggly could bring help.

The sneaky cats had pulled their prisoners down a dark alley, loaded them onto a dinghy, and locked them in the stinky brig at the bottom of the *Nine Lives*. The kitten pirates had also stolen Steak-Eye's bag of meat. Wally hadn't yet decided which was worse: being catnapped, or having to tell Steak-Eye they had lost his juicy steaks.

The brig was small, and the kitten ship

smelled like tuna and hair balls. *Cat* hair balls.
The combination of the tight space and the smell
was driving Spike crazy. He dashed around the
tiny cell, his feet flying in all directions. Then he

pawed at the metal bars, trying to climb them.

Puggly watched the chubby bulldog curiously. "He's doin' a brig jig," she said, giggling.

"What's a brig jig?" Wally asked.

Puggly sneezed. "I made it up. It looks like Spike's trying to dance his way out of jail. Dancin' a jig in the brig. *Brig jig.*" Puggly waited for someone to laugh, but no one was in much of a laughing mood. Finally, she whispered, "*Piggly* would think it's funny."

When he got tired of climbing the walls, Spike tried digging a hole in the solid floor below their feet. When that didn't work, either, he began to wail. Big, sad sobs that echoed around them.

"Piggly went for help, Spike," Wally reminded him. "I'm sure our crew is just trying to come up with a plan for how to sneak on board to steal us back."

The *Nine Lives* rocked and swayed. It lurched. Spike, who was now curled into a chubby ball, began to roll around the floor like a giant bug.

"In case you were wondering?" Henry said quietly. "The ship's moving."

"Moving?" Spike shot up and ran in circles. "If we be moving, Captain Red Beard and the others are never going to get to us! Never!"

"Silence!" Lucinda the Loud hissed. No one had heard her coming. The longhaired kitten captain stood in shadow nearby, her fluffy tail swishing silently. A smaller tabby cat stood at her side. The two Siamese kittens paced nearby, grinning.

Spike tried hiding under Wally. But he was far too big to fit.

"Allow me to introduce myself!" Lucinda the Loud boomed. "I am Lucinda the Loud, the captain of the kitten pirates." Her fierce green

eyes focused on Henry. "And you ... are the funniest-looking dog I have ever seen."

Wally stepped forward and said, "Henry's a boy, ma'am. My best mate, and one of the finest pirates in all the world."

"I do not know this breed you call boy!" shouted Lucinda the Loud.

The tabby cat whispered something in her ear.

Lucinda boomed, "Speak up, Fluffy!"

The cat called Fluffy sighed. "It's Fluffy the Claw. *The Claw!* If you insist on calling yourself Lucinda the Loud, please call me the Claw. Skip the Fluffy part, please." The tabby cat shook his head. "And, Captain, a boy is not a breed of dog. It's a human."

"Ah, yes!" shouted Lucinda the Loud. "I see, Fluffy. A human dog. *Human-dog. Hu-dog.* For short, I shall call it a *hog!*" She stared at Henry for another minute, then continued, "Now, in case it is not clear: you are our prisoners. We have sent a message in a bottle to your captain. If he wants to get his pups and his hog back again, he must turn over his jewels and maps. And your softest beds. All the best loot."

"Not my bed!" Spike cried.

Puggly growled. "You can't do this."

"Ah!" meowed Lucinda the Loud. "I already have. The message went doodly-doodly-doo, floating all across the waves. Your ship got our message. The puppy pirate crew has until tomorrow to give us their loot. Or we'll show you what kitten pirates do with dogs." She turned to Fluffy. "I forget, what exactly do we do with dogs?"

Fluffy whispered something in her ear.

Lucinda screeched, "You know I can't hear you when you whisper, Fluffy!"

The kitten pirate captain turned and pranced out of the brig. Fluffy followed. The Siamese cats giggled and slunk after them. They winked at the prisoners just before the door slammed shut.

The puppy pirates were alone again. Trapped.

Wally stood and turned to his friends. "We can't let Captain Red Beard get bossed around by a bunch of *cats*!"

"How are we supposed to stop them?" Spike asked in a shaky voice.

"I hate to admit it, but Spike's got a point," said Puggly.

"In case you were wondering, I don't think our crew can help us now," Henry said.

Wally took a deep breath. "Henry's right. That's why . . ." He looked long and hard at Spike, Puggly, and Henry. "Mates, we are going to rescue ourselves!"

The Brains of the Boat

A moment later, Fluffy the Claw stepped softly back into the room. "Ahoy," the quiet tabby cat purred.

None of the puppy pirates said anything.

"What do you want, *Fluffy*?" Puggly finally grumbled. "Shouldn't you be busy taking a cat-nap or licking your fur or something?"

The small tabby spoke softly. "As the ship's first mate, I wanted to offer my apology." Even

Spike perked up a bit when he heard that. "And you may call me the Claw. Skip the Fluffy, if you please."

"Does your captain know you're here?" Wally asked.

"Captain Lucinda the Loud doesn't know much," said the Claw. Then he looked sorry he'd said it out loud. "Let's keep that a secret between us."

Puggly laughed. "Sounds a lot like a captain we know." She cocked her head at the tabby cat. "Are you like our first mate, Curly, then? The brains of the boat?"

"You could say that, yes," the Claw purred. "My noble captain and I do not agree on everything. Today, we do not agree about what to do with you, our prisoners. I would like to set sail for the South Seas, on our next adventure. But my captain wants to play this silly game of cat and mouse with your ship. I think this is a waste of our time."

"We agree!" barked Wally. "Maybe if you just let us out of here, we could both be on our way."

The Claw paced back and forth, his tail flipping to and fro. On the end of his tail was a ring with a key. He dangled it in front of the prison bars. It was almost close enough to touch. "Perhaps I should do just that. . . ."

"Please, Fluffy. *The Claw,* sir," Wally said, feeling a tiny spark of hope. "Think of the wonderful adventures waiting for you in the South Seas. We were just there, and it was so nice."

"Very pretty," Spike offered.

"It's beautiful this time of year," Puggly added.

The Claw lifted his paw and licked it. "Even if I were to let you out of here, you'd still be trapped on the ship. How would you—" He cut himself off as the door flew open. A matted orange cat leaped into the room and yelled, "Fluffy, there's trouble above deck. Catnip!"

The Claw swung around and glared at the orange cat. "It's *the Claw*! And *how*, exactly, did catnip land on our ship?"

The orange cat looked scared. "Uh, Moopsy and Boopsy brought a whole crate of catnip-filled toys on board. I don't know what those two naughty kittens were planning to do with them."

"Where's the crate now?" the Claw hissed.

"I got it away from the twins," said the orange cat. "It's right out there."

"In the hallway?" the Claw meowed. "Where anyone could find it? If the rest of the crew gets hold of those toys, they will all leave their posts! Our whole ship will be chaos!"

"What should we do?" the orange cat asked.

The Claw went still as a statue, thinking. Finally, he said, "I'll hide the crate in the galley. No one but Hook the Cook goes in there, and he can't see or smell anything. Besides, the stink of his cookin' will mask the scent of catnip. As soon as we dock again, those toys are going heave-ho!"

"Aye, aye, Fluffy!" said the orange cat. "Uh, I mean, the Claw."

"Wait!" Wally yipped as the Claw and the orange cat turned to leave. "Don't forget about—" The kittens rushed out. The door slammed behind them. "Us."

"Nooooooo!" Spike moaned. "We were so close to getting out of here. *This* close." He held his paws together. "This . . ." *Sob*. "Close." *Snuffle*.

"It's okay," Wally said. He sounded more

confident than he felt. "We're gonna find some way out of here. I'm sure of it!"

"Does that mean you have an idea?" Puggly said hopefully.

Wally hung his head. "Not yet."

"In case you were wondering, mates? I have good news," Henry said. "Who wants to get back to the *Salty Bone*?"

"Maybe you should remind your boy that we're locked in," Puggly snorted. "Fluffy just hightailed it out of here without unlocking our cell."

Henry held out a fist. He opened his fingers. Something small and golden gleamed in his palm.

Spike danced his brig jig. "We're freeeeeee!"

Wally woofed, "Is that what I think it is?"

It was. Henry had the key. "Cats may be sneaky, but I'm sneakier," he said, grinning.

"That tabby cat didn't even notice when I reached right through the bars and grabbed the key off his tail. Only one thing to do now." He twisted the key in the lock, and something clicked. The door of their jail cell swung open. Henry waved his hand toward Puggly and said, "Ladies first."

The Digging Room

They marched out of the open cell door. Everyone's spirits were lifted. But outside the brig, all four of them stopped. They glanced left, then right. The puppy pirates weren't locked up anymore. But they were still lost on an enemy ship in the middle of the ocean—surrounded by kittens.

Spike whimpered. "What now?"

"Maybe we could try to swim away?" Puggly suggested.

Wally gulped. No way would he swim in the

ocean. There was nothing safe about that. But before he had to say it, Henry blurted out, "In case you were wondering, the best way to escape a pirate ship is to hop in a dinghy."

"Aye! Let's get above deck and find a dinghy. We can row home," Wally said happily. He loved dinghies. They were the little wooden boats that hung off the side of the ship. Just that morning, Henry had rowed one from the *Salty Bone* to shore. Morning seemed like a *very* long time ago now.

Henry rubbed his chin and added, "We have to remember, mates: the most important rule of being a prisoner on an enemy ship is to remain calm. Even if the cats are on our tail, we can't let them scare us!"

Wally woofed his agreement. "Aye!"

Puggly flapped her cape and growled, "They can't scare me."

"Nope, no thanks, not going to happen." Spike backed into a corner. "I'll just stay in the brig, if that's okay?"

"Spike," grumbled Puggly, "didn't you hear what the boy said? We need to remain calm and *not* let them scare us."

"Uh-huh," Spike whimpered. "Calm . . . cats . . . no scare . . . no fear." He started shaking his head, hard. "No *way*! These are *kittens* you're talking about! They're fierce beasts."

Puggly giggled. "Aw, they're just a bunch of pussycats. Your paw's bigger than ol' Fluffy's head."

Wally stood before the big bulldog. "And remember: we're your crew, Spike. You can trust us, can't you? We'll get you out of here safely."

"You promise?" Spike asked in a tiny voice.

Wally couldn't promise—because he *wasn't* sure. But he was sure they couldn't leave Spike behind. And they couldn't stay in the brig forever. "I promise to try my best," said Wally. "We all will. We'll be back on board the *Salty Bone* in no time. You'll see. We can do it."

They all held their breath, waiting to see if Spike would go for it. Spike sighed. Then he heaved himself off the floor and said, "Okay, mates. I'm in."

Together, the prisoners tiptoed through the enemy ship. They poked their noses into dark hallways and small rooms, trying to find their way above deck.

The floors on the *Nine Lives* were made of wood, just like on the *Salty Bone,* but they were not nearly as scratched up. Tiny bells and stuffed mice hung from the ceilings. The walls were covered with a rough carpet that looked like it had done battle with hundreds of cat claws.

Unlike the *Salty Bone,* which had wide hallways, open spaces, and large rooms, the kitten

ship was a maze of tight spaces and little cub-
bies. Every hall had many other corridors leading off of it. Most of the cabins were small and
squeezy, just big enough for one or two cats to
curl up in. There were rooms stacked on top of
rooms. Henry had to duck and crawl in many
spots to make it through.

Finally, a winding hallway dead-ended in
a large cabin. Its door was unlocked. "No one
in here," Puggly said, poking her snout inside.
"But it sure smells pretty. Like roses and per-
fume and a warm spring day."

"The whole room is filled with sand!" Spike
cried. Forgetting his fear, the big bulldog rushed
through the doorway and into the room. "Mates!
Lookie. The cats have a digging room. We need
a digging room. How great would it be if we
had a digging room?" He quickly set to work
making a giant hole in the center of the sand.

Meanwhile, Puggly sniffed around the edges

of the room. "I'm trying to find what smells so pretty. I think they're hiding something pugglorious in here! If it be jewels, I'll find it!"

Henry looked amused. "Um, mates? In case you were wondering, this is the cats' litter box. It's where they, uh . . . do their business."

"Pay bills and stuff?" asked Spike. He curled up to rest in his hole in the sand.

Henry's face turned red as he went on.

"Okay, so you don't seem to get that, do you? Let me say it like this. . . . You know how dogs like to go on trees? Well, cats like to go in sand. Sand just like this."

"This sand is their potty?" Spike shrieked. He scurried up and shook off. "Cats. Pee. In. This. Sand?"

"Shiver me timbers, they sure do make it smell beautiful," said Puggly. She hustled back out to the corridor. "Ah, well. Moving on!"

But no matter which direction they turned, they couldn't find their way up to the deck. It felt like they had been searching forever when they heard the *click-clack* of tiny claws against the wooden floor right around a corner. Someone was coming!

The puppies froze.

"What do you think the captain will do to the puppy pirate prisoners when she finds them?" a soft voice purred.

"The same thing she'll do to us if we *don't* find them," another voice answered.

"In case you were wondering?" Henry whispered. "I think now might be a good time to hide."

They moved very quickly but *very* quietly. Moments later, the four friends slipped through an unlocked door farther down the hallway. Henry eased the door closed behind them. Wally wagged his tail. Spike trembled in relief.

"Safe," Puggly said. "For now."

They turned around, and their eyes went wide.

A human girl glared back at them. "What, exactly, do you think you're doing in my cabin?"

Prove Yourself a Pirate

"You're a girl," Henry said. "What are you doing on a kitten ship?"

"You're a *boy*," she pointed out. A tiny gray kitten peeked out from under the girl's blanket and blinked sleepily at the intruders. "What are *you* doing on a kitten ship? With a bunch of"— she glanced at Wally, Puggly, and Spike— "dogs? And whatever you call that little wrinkled creature wearing a scarf?"

"I'm a pug, lady," snarled Puggly. "And this here is me cape!"

They could hear the muffled sound of cat paws padding past on the other side of the door. Henry put his finger to his lips and whispered, "Listen, we've been catnapped. The kittens on this ship are after us. Please, can we just hang out in here until the coast is clear? We don't want to cause any problems. We just want to get back to our own ship."

The girl curled her lip. "Are you asking me to hide you?"

"Yeah, I guess I am." Henry shrugged. "What's your name, anyway?"

"Ruby," the girl said, her eyes narrowed. The tiny gray kitten leaped onto her shoulder, where it perched like a parrot. "Ruby the Brave. And this is Pete the Mighty." She rubbed Pete's cheek. The kitten had already fallen back to sleep, curled around Ruby's neck.

"Ha!" Henry laughed. "Mighty? *That* little ball of fuzz?"

The girl slipped past him. She reached for the door handle. "Want to make fun of us, huh? Go ahead. I'll just let my crew know where you are."

Wally barked in alarm, "Don't do that! He's sorry. Right, Henry? Aren't you sorry?"

Henry grabbed her arm. "I'm sorry I made fun of your cat's name. Will you still help us?" he said quickly. "In case you were wondering, my name's Henry. Just Henry."

"Well, in case *you* were wondering?" said Ruby. "All the best pirates have two names."

"Oh, yeah? What do you know about pirates?" Henry asked.

"Everything," announced Ruby.

Henry shook his head. "Everything, huh? Not as much as me, I bet."

Ruby glared at Henry. "What are you doing with the puppy pirate ship, anyway? Why would you want to hang around with a pack of scurvy dogs?"

"They're my mates!" Henry snapped. "It's a long story."

"Were you a stowaway?" Ruby asked, petting

her kitten. "Pete the Mighty and I were stow-aways together." The tiny gray kitten purred in his sleep.

Henry rested his hand on Wally's head. "Well, *we* were even better stowaways."

Ruby and Henry glared at each other.

Puggly rolled her eyes. "Maybe these two should write each other letters and argue about all of this once we get out of here," she grumbled to Wally. "But for now, do you think your human can just focus on getting this lass to help us off this ship?"

"So you want my help, do you, *Just* Henry?" Ruby sighed. "First, I dare you to prove you're a worthy pirate."

"Ask me anything," Henry blurted. "I can prove it."

"Okay," she said, thinking. "Do you know what a ship's kitchen is called?"

Henry laughed. "Are you kidding me? It's

the galley. In case you were wondering, that's simple."

Ruby smirked. "What's another name for a pirate's sword?"

"A cutlass!" Henry said proudly. "Or a nimcha, or a scimitar, or—"

"Okay, okay." Ruby nodded. "Do you know why a lot of human pirates have pierced ears?"

Henry jutted out his chin. "Simple. It's because they think it improves their eyesight."

"Is that true?" Puggly whispered to Wally, pawing at her earrings. "No wonder I can see so well in the dark!"

Ruby narrowed her eyes and grinned. "I've got one more for you. I hope you like riddles. What's a pirate's favorite letter?"

Puggly, Spike, and Wally all exchanged a confused look.

But Henry didn't look at all worried. "*R*. As

in, *arrrrrrr*!" He grinned. "But in case you were wondering, that's not a riddle. It's a joke."

"Congratulations. You got them all right," Ruby said. "But if you actually knew anything about pirates, you would know you should never trust your enemy." She flung open the door to her quarters and screamed, "Here, kitty, kitties! The prisoners are in here!"

Cooking Up a Plan

Wally, Spike, Puggly, and Henry dashed through the kitten ship's winding corridors, trying to escape. Hundreds of feet padded behind them. The kittens were closing in. The ship was filled with angry hissing and meowing.

All the twisty hallways and small rooms made it easier for the puppy pirate team to stay ahead of the cats. But after a while, Wally slowed to a walk. "We'll never get off this ship if we keep having to run and hide," he said, panting. "We need a better plan."

Spike whined, "But these are *cats*! Mean, hissing, horrible beasts. We've got to hide, mates. They scare me."

"We have to figure out a smart way to fight back," Wally said.

"There are four of us and a whole ship full of furballs," Puggly noted. "We can't fight. We'd be doomed."

Wally sniffed the air. "Do you smell something strange?"

Puggly snorted. "Yeah, cat puke. Or cat food. They smell the same to me."

"The galley!" Wally yelped. He suddenly remembered something the Claw had said back in the brig. And it gave him an idea. "We have to find the galley."

Before the others could ask questions, Wally

was off. He followed his nose. He sniffed until he found a door that opened into a small, hot room that smelled even *more* like cat than the rest of the ship did.

Spike licked his chops. "Smells kind of yummy. I'm so hungry."

"Looks like we found the galley, mates," Henry whispered. The walls were lined with crates of canned cat food and boxes filled with smoked tuna.

Spike shuddered. "Yuck! Cat food? I can't believe I thought it smelled good in here."

It did kind of smell like Steak-Eye's stew in the kitten ship galley. Wally giggled. He was the only pup on their crew who knew about Steak-Eye's secret ingredient: Kitty Kibble. Wally's tummy growled. It had been hours since their last meal!

"Why did you want to find the galley, Wally?" Puggly asked, poking her nose under a tall table. "Are you thinking they hid Steak-Eye's stolen bag of steaks in here?"

In fact, Wally wasn't thinking about food at all. He was pretty sure the key to his plan was hidden somewhere in this room. "Remember when Fluffy the Claw said no one ever comes in here? That it was a good place to hide things?"

"You think I was listening to that furball?" Puggly said.

Wally sniffed around the edges of the room,

following a strange scent. Finally, he found what he was looking for. A huge cardboard box. "It's here!" he ruffed.

"You found the steaks?" Puggly barked, running over.

Henry peered into the box and gasped. "This is a box of catnip toys!"

"Aye," said Wally. "The Claw hid them here, because he knew what would happen if the crew got their claws on them!" He looked at the others to see if they had caught on.

"Are you thinking what I'm thinking?" Puggly said happily. "Prank time?"

"Well . . . sort of," Wally said.

"*Arr-arr-arooo!*" Puggly woofed.

Wally nudged the box of catnip toys out from under the table. "Remember when the Claw said that if the kitten pirates got ahold of the catnip toys they would all leave their posts? He said there would be chaos on the ship."

"Aye," Puggly snorted.

"We should distract the cats with the catnip!" Henry said, clapping. "Escape while the enemy is playing."

Wally woofed, "Exactly."

Spike looked hopeful. "Maybe this box of toys will keep the cats busy enough that we can finally get out of here."

Henry lifted the box. The four friends hurried through the maze of the kitten ship. Every time they heard kitten claws closing in on them, Henry dropped one of the toys.

The pups heard the kittens mewing with delight and pawing at the toys behind them. The plan was working!

"I smell fresh air!" Wally said, rounding a corner. "Mates—stairs!"

The pups raced each other to the top of a long staircase. They gulped in breaths of salty air. Way over on the starboard side of the ship,

two kitten pirates were swabbing the deck. Other than those two, the coast was clear.

"Yo ho haroo!" howled Spike, running to the deck rail.

"Shhh!" Puggly shushed him. She pointed to the horizon and whispered, "Look over yonder. I see the *Salty Bone!*"

"Our friends are coming to rescue us!" Wally barked.

Puggly put her paws on the rail. She peered over the edge and wagged her curly tail. "There's a dinghy!"

Dangling from the railing at the other end of the boat was a small dinghy, just big enough for a crew of four. "To the dinghy!" urged Henry, running toward it.

"*Meow!*" Before they could reach the escape boat, a hiss sliced through the air. "Kittens, all claws on deck. The puppy pirates are trying to get away!"

Ready Oar Not

"Run!" Spike yowled. "Kitty attack!"

"No more running," Wally said firmly as kitten pirates swarmed the deck. "It's time to show these cats what puppy pirates are made of."

"It is?" Spike asked, trying to hide behind Puggly. But since Puggly was the size of Spike's head, she wasn't a great cover.

"It is," Wally said. He stood tall and proud. "Are you ready to get off this ship?"

"Um, yes?" Spike didn't sound very sure. But he slowly got back on his feet and stood beside Wally.

"We can do this, Spike," Wally said.

Spike was shaking with fear. They were surrounded.

Wally barked at Puggly, "Ready?"

"Fun time!" Puggly yipped. She wound her squat body between Henry's legs, jumped up on her hind legs, and knocked the box out of Henry's hands. The catnip-filled toys fanned out across the deck. "Here, kitty, kitty!"

Every cat on board shrieked. There was a tangle of claws and tails as the kittens fought over the toys. Moopsy and Boopsy batted a toy chili pepper back and forth.

There weren't enough toys for everyone, so the kitten pirates played tug-of-war. In no time, half the toys had been torn open. The air was filled with swirling, whirling flakes of catnip.

Fluffy the Claw pounced on a toy fish. "Stop it!" he hissed at himself. "Stop it, the Claw! You're setting a bad example!" But the catnip was too wonderful for even the first mate to resist.

"Stand guard!" Lucinda the Loud shouted, hissing at her crew for order. But soon the catnip tempted even the captain. She grabbed the toy chili pepper from Moopsy and Boopsy, and her body began to wiggle.

"Kittens!" Ruby the Brave screamed. "The puppy pirates are getting away!"

While the cats played, Henry and the puppy pirates wove a path across the deck, through the catnip-crazy kittens. No one stopped them as they climbed into the dinghy.

Henry began to let the rope out on the dinghy, lowering their escape boat toward the water. In the distance, the *Salty Bone* was cutting through the rough seas.

"Not so fast," Ruby the Brave said, leaning over the deck rail. She put her foot on the rope. The dinghy was stuck. It dangled halfway between the ship's main deck and the sea. Ruby smirked. "You're not going anywhere. Doggies, stay!"

Ruby and Henry stared each other down. Suddenly, Moopsy and Boopsy leaped onto Ruby's head. She shrieked, "What are you cats doing?"

Puggly glanced up. "What *are* they doing?"

Ruby's voice was muffled by two fluffy kitten tails. "Get off me!" she cried. "I can't see anything. The puppy pirates are going to escape."

"You heard her," Moopsy and Boopsy purred at Wally and his friends. "Go. Escape."

"Wait, you're helping us?" Wally asked. "But you're kitten pirates."

"We're helping *you*, pup," the Siamese twins meowed at Wally. "Because you helped us on the dock this morning. You stopped that puggy prank. Cats are nothing if not fair. We always repay our debts."

Henry took his chance while Ruby's face was covered in fur. He tugged at the rope again. He lowered their boat the rest of the way to the water. "See you again someday, Ruby the Brave." Henry lifted his hand in a salute as their dinghy floated away from the *Nine Lives*.

Moopsy and Boopsy hopped off Ruby's head. "You can bet on it!" Ruby shouted back at Henry.

The dinghy rocked and rolled on the waves. Henry reached for the oars. But a wave made the boat sway, and he tripped over Spike.

Knocked off balance, Spike tumbled into Puggly.

Puggly knocked against Wally.

And Wally bumped into the oar . . . just hard enough to knock it over the side of the dinghy. The oar splashed into the water.

Henry lunged for it, but the oar slipped out

of his grip. It floated out of reach, bouncing along on the waves.

They were stranded.

"In case you were wondering? You can't row a boat with only one oar," Henry said with a sigh.

"What are we going to do now?" Spike cried. "Bulldogs can't swim! I sink like a stone."

Puggly flopped onto the bottom of the boat. "I can swim a little, but there's no way I would make it all the way to the *Salty Bone*. Me legs are too short."

Wally gulped. He had an idea, but it scared him. "I could try to fetch the oar."

"Well, there you go," Puggly said happily. "You're a retriever. You were born to fetch!"

Wally shivered. He dunked his paw into the water. It was so cold and so, so wet. The sea was gray and huge and scary-looking. Could he do it? "I . . . ," Wally began. He pulled his paw away from the ocean waves. How could he tell his crew he was too scared to save them?

"You don't have to do it if you're afraid," Spike whispered. "I never do anything I'm scared of."

Wally looked at his friend and shook his head. "That's not true, Spike. You've been doing things you're scared of all day."

Spike sniffed. "Only because you told me I could! And because you promised to help me."

"I said you could because I *knew* you could, Spike," said Wally. "You're big, and you're tough. You could do almost anything you wanted if you tried."

"Well, gosh . . . when you put it that way," Spike said, sitting up tall. "I guess I am big and strong. I was born tough, just like you were born to swim."

Watching Spike puff out his chest with

pride made Wally smile. It also made him feel
sure. Just because he was afraid didn't mean he
couldn't do it. He had swum once. He probably
could do it again. "I'm going to get that oar."

Wally took a deep breath. Then he leaped
into the freezing-cold ocean.

Hair Ball Horror

The water felt like ice on Wally's skin. But it was easier to paddle than he thought it would be. He felt bouncy and light, almost like he was a boat floating on the rolling waves. He breathed through his nose, careful not to open his mouth to let in any of the salty sea water.

With his friends cheering for him in the little dinghy, Wally paddled through the waves. His legs were strong and sure. He reached the oar in no time. He wrapped his mouth around the handle and began to swim back. Again, he was careful not to breathe through his mouth. This was harder to do now that he was towing something.

"You can do it, mate!" Henry screamed. "Fetch, boy."

"Our hero," barked Spike.

"Yo ho ho, mighty pirate," arfed Puggly.

Wally's legs were growing tired. But he was almost there.

"Got it!" Henry shouted, reaching into the water to grab the oar out of Wally's mouth.

As Henry settled back into the boat, Spike reached his mouth over the side and pulled Wally out of the water by the scruff of his neck. "You okay?" he asked.

Wally shook off. "Yes," he barked. And he was. He was more than okay. Because this time, swimming hadn't left him shaky and scared. This time, he came out of the water feeling like a hero. He had done it!

Henry sat on a small bench in the center of the boat. He pulled the oars through the water. But as they began to move toward the *Salty Bone,* something flew through the air at the dinghy. It landed in the water. *Plop.*

Another. *Plip.*

Another. *Plunk.*

Spike screeched and hid under Henry's legs. "The kittens are shootin' cannonballs at us. Row faster." He clawed at Henry's legs.

Plip. Plop. Splash.

"What in the . . . ?" Puggly ruffed. "Those aren't cannonballs! They're throwin' *hair balls.*" She giggled. "That is disgusting . . . and clever."

Wally barked, urging Henry to go faster.

The kittens launched hair ball after hair ball. Whenever one landed in the boat, Spike yelped and swatted it back out.

Soon they were far enough from the kitten ship that the hair balls couldn't reach them anymore. Ahead, they could see their friends on the main deck of the *Salty Bone*.

Curly was at the top of the crow's nest. Her tiny voice rang out loud and clear, "Ahoy, mateys!"

The whole crew worked together to pull the dinghy out of the water. The four friends tumbled out of their tiny boat and onto the deck of the *Salty Bone*. The rest of the puppy pirates surrounded them, barking a welcome.

"It's great to be home!" Wally said.

Piggly ran over to greet her sister. The two pugs wrestled and giggled as Puggly told Piggly all about their adventures on the *Nine Lives*.

Steak-Eye trotted over to the pug twins. "Where are me steaks?" he growled at Puggly.

She eyed him but said nothing.

Steak-Eye snapped, "Lost 'em, eh?"

Piggly and Puggly waited for the cook to explode with anger.

Instead, Steak-Eye laughed. "Guess that means I'll have eight extra paws in the kitchen for the next few weeks. Piggly and Puggly, report for duty in the galley tomorrow morning before the sun comes up."

Puggly groaned. But Piggly grinned. "Fine with me. Kitchen duty means more snacks!"

"In case you were wondering?" Henry told the rest of the crew. "You've got to be one tough pirate to escape a catnapping!"

Spike nodded. "A mighty tough pirate." He yawned, then tucked his tail between his legs. "And this tough guy is headed to bed. I'm going

to curl up for a nice, long nap. Bravery is tiring!"
He slipped away.

Captain Red Beard growled, "We need to figure out how to get revenge on those frisky cats."

Piggly and Puggly cheered.

"Revenge!" Puggly shouted. "I've got lots of ideas for you, Captain."

Old Salt stepped forward. "Consider your next step carefully, Captain."

"Why?" Red Beard said, looking down at his feet. "Am I going to step in something sticky?"

"I just mean, maybe it's best to end this here," said Old Salt. "Don't go looking for more trouble."

Wally nodded. As much as he loved battles and adventures, the only thing he wanted now was a little nap. He had spent enough time with the kitten pirates to last him for a good,

long while. He yawned, then curled up beside
Henry. On the horizon, they could see the
kitten ship sailing into the setting sun.

Captain Red Beard howled, "Don't go

lookin' for trouble?" Then he grumbled, "But I'm a pirate. Trouble is my middle name."

"Then let's set sail for our next adventure," Old Salt said with a smile. "We can wait for trouble to find us. It always does."

Puppy Pirates
Sea Sick
Even pirate captains have sick days. . . .
Erin Soderberg

For Henry, who asked me to write him
an adventure series...I hope this one
keeps you entertained on *your* sick
days, buddy.
—E.S.

 CONTENTS

Pirate Day Prep

"*Yo ho ho and a bundle of beef! Yo ho ho and a lottle of fun!*" Captain Red Beard danced across the deck of his ship. He was singing a silly, happy tune. "*I love my ship and I love my crew, but I'm still number one!*"

None of the puppy pirates on board the *Salty Bone* was used to seeing their captain so jolly. Usually, the scraggly terrier was pretty gruff. But Captain Red Beard's favorite holiday, Party Like a Pirate Day, was just one day away.

He couldn't leash in his excitement.

"All paws on deck," the captain ordered, his tail wagging happily. "Time to prepare for our world-famous Party Like a Pirate Day banquet!"

A cuddly golden retriever pup named Wally skidded across the deck. He stood at attention. "Aye, aye, Captain," Wally barked. "I am ready to help."

"Excellent, little Walty," Red Beard said. The captain patted Wally's head with one of his scraggly paws. "Good boy."

Wally's fluffy tail swished back and forth. He loved when Captain Red Beard was pleased with him. As the newest member of the puppy pirate crew, Wally was always working hard to show the captain he deserved his bunk on board the ship. Wally's best mate, a boy named Henry, joined Wally and the dozens of other pups gathered around the captain.

"Listen up, crew!" Red Beard ordered. "Party Like a Pirate Day is tomorrow. As you all know, the Pirate Day party is absotootly the bestest event of the whole year."

The puppy pirates cheered. No one was more excited than Wally. This was his first Party Like a Pirate Day. He had heard plenty of stories about past parties from his pug friends, Piggly and Puggly. Piggly spun in happy circles when she told him about the food and treats the captain saved for the party. Puggly's favorite part was getting to skip chores to play games and sing songs.

"Everything about Pirate Day has to be perfecto-nino," the captain said. "We have much to prepare. As always, my plans for the party are written in a secret code. We don't want those furball kitten pirates to find our Pirate Day plans and steal them. Aye?"

The puppy pirates all cheered again. "Aye, aye, Captain!"

Curly, the ship's first mate, stepped forward. The poufy white mini poodle whispered, "Excuse me, Captain. You do remember how to crack your codes, though . . . correct?"

"Of course I do not remember how to crack my codes, Curly!" Captain Red Beard snapped. "What would be the point of a secret code if it's not a secret? As soon as I write 'em, I forget 'em. But I have the handy-dandy code cracker right here." The captain picked up a sheet of parchment with his mouth. He unrolled it and waved it in the air.

Henry squinted to try to make out some of the words on the piece of parchment. He read aloud: *"Party Like a Pirate Day Code Sheet: Top Secret."* Henry leaned toward Wally and whispered, "Hey, mate, we should get our hands on that! I love cracking codes."

Red Beard pushed the paper to the side and continued his speech. "I hope everyone remembers the most important rule of Pirate Day. On this super-de-dooper holiday, we do everything my way. Whatever I say goes. After all, the captain is the most important part of any pirate ship, am I right?"

Curly began, "But, Captain—"

"No buts," Red Beard said, stomping. "I get to decide everything! I'm in charge, and that's final."

Curly nodded but spoke again. "Captain, it's just that the crew has a few ideas for how to make this the best Pirate Day party yet. If only you would let us—"

"Enough!" Red Beard snapped. "I wrote up the plans for the party. Your job is to follow them. Understood?" He looked around, but no one dared say anything. "Now, pups, let's see what our first order of business is." He padded over to a list of instructions that were posted on the wall. Then he glanced down at his code sheet. "First, pups, we need to blow up balloons. Fill your bodies with wind and *puff puff puff*!"

The puppies all scrambled to grab balloons. They huffed and puffed, filling balloons quicker than Henry could tie them closed. Soon they had filled a huge crate with balloons of many colors. The captain lifted a yellow balloon out of the crate. He bopped it into the air and chased after it.

Other pups did the same. There were more than a dozen balloons bopping around.

Bop.

Bop.

Pop!

The yellow balloon popped. Red Beard yelped and jumped a foot into the air.

Pop! Across the deck, a red balloon popped.

Spike, a nervous bulldog, hid from the loud noise.

Pop! A green balloon burst, and Olly the beagle howled.

Wally spotted Piggly and Puggly giggling on the other side of the deck. As usual, the pugs were making mischief. The silly pug twins had loaded up a bamboo shooter with crunchy treats and were aiming them at the balloons.

Whenever one of the treats hit a balloon, it popped.

Red Beard spotted them. "Enough!" he barked. "This is no time for your nonsense, pugs." Red Beard scanned the crowd of pups on the deck. His eyes narrowed. "Some of my pups are missing," he growled. "Where is Steak-Eye?"

Wally looked around, searching for the ship's cranky cook.

Curly stepped forward. "Sir, Steak-Eye is feeling ill."

"Ill? What do you mean?" Captain Red Beard growled, searching the crowd again. "And Old Salt?"

"Also sick," Curly said. "There's a bug going around—sneezy noses and the stomach flea. It's taken down half the crew. Otis and Marshmallow and Paco and Puck and—"

"A *bug*?" Captain Red Beard shrieked.

"What kind of bug? We will fight it! Puppy pirates are larger and stronger than fleas. We can take it out lickety-split!"

"Not a *bug* bug, Captain," Curly gently explained. "They're sick. Unwell."

Red Beard howled. "Sickness is not allowed on Party Like a Pirate Day! Only partying! That is an order! It—it—it—it—"

Captain Red Beard's nose twitched. His whiskers trembled. His eyes squeezed shut. He sniffled. He snuffed. And then, with a mighty *ah-choo,* Captain Red Beard sneezed.

Sneezy Wheezy
Captain Queasy

"Ohhhhhh," Captain Red Beard groaned. "My head. My tongue. My paws. My nose. Everything hurts." He sneezed. He wheezed. He whined. He moaned.

The captain was tucked into bed under a heavy green blanket. Curly, Wally, Henry, and the pugs crowded around him. "What can we do for you, Captain?" Curly asked. "How can we help you feel better?"

Wally could see that Curly was sick, too—sick with worry. With the captain stuck in bed, the ship was now Curly's to run. But with the Pirate Day party to prepare, and half the crew sick in bed, *and* the usual pirate ship tasks, Wally guessed Curly was nervous about getting everything done. Wally knew she could do it. The poodle was smart and fierce, and the whole crew trusted her.

"Ice," Red Beard wheezed. "Fresh ice and the blue blanket. I like the blue blankie."

Wally ripped the green blanket off the captain's body. Curly tucked him in again—this time with the blue blanket. "Better?"

"Red. It's actually the red blanket I like," Red Beard whined.

But once he was tucked into the red blanket, he didn't like that one, either. Next it was blue again, then green, red, polka dot, black fleece, fur. . . . Finally, the captain settled on a purple-and-gold plaid blanket. He took a deep, wheezing breath. "Party Like a Pirate Day will be ruined," the captain sobbed. "The best day of the year. I've waited three hundred and ninety-two days since the last Pirate Day!"

"You mean three hundred and sixty-five?" Curly said gently. "Pirate Day comes around once a year. That's every three hundred and sixty-five days, Captain."

"As I was saying, I have waited three hundred and sixty-five days for this. And now, sick!" Red Beard cried. "Sick with the sneezies and a stomach flea. What will we do?"

"You need not worry, Captain," Curly said. "As your trusty first mate, I will make sure the ship is ready for the party tomorrow."

"Impossible!" Red Beard sneezed, then wiped his drippy nose on the blanket. "I'm the only one who can do it. Without me in charge, Pirate Day is ruined."

"It's not!" Wally yelped. He hated to see the captain so upset. "Curly can do it. And we'll all help her."

"Listen to the little pup," Curly told the captain. "I can handle this."

The captain's eyes drooped. He was nearly asleep. "You promise?"

"You can count on us, Captain." Curly looked to Wally and the others. They all nodded. "We'll follow your orders and throw you the best Pirate Day party ever."

Captain Red Beard sighed. "I don't see how that's possible. But you can try." He reached his muzzle under the blanket and grabbed something in his teeth. "Here is my Party Like a Pirate Day Top-Secret Code Sheet. You can use it to decode my instructions. But please, keep it safe. It's the only copy."

"Of course," Curly said. "We'll get to work right away."

"Arrrrr!" Captain Red Beard cried out suddenly. "I have an itch!"

"Where?" Curly asked, dropping the code sheet to the floor. "Would you like me to scratch it for you before I go?"

Red Beard whimpered. "Yes. My ear. The lefty one."

Curly used her paw to scratch at the captain's ear. After a good, long scratch, she hopped off his bed and made her way toward the door. "Crew, follow me. We must get to work on the party plans at once."

"Curly?" Red Beard croaked. "Please don't go. Stay with me. What if I need something?"

Wally stepped forward. "Sir, I could stay here and take care of you. Curly has a crew to run and a ship to steer."

"And Piggly and I would be happy to start working on the party," said Puggly. She shot her sister a sly look.

Captain Red Beard burrowed under his covers and whined. "But I need Curly. She's my first mate. I must have her by my side." He looked at Curly with his saddest puppy-dog eyes. "Please?

You can run the ship and plan the party from here."

Curly sighed. "If you need me, I'll stay."

The captain yawned, then fell fast asleep. Curly turned to the others. "Wally, take the captain's code cracker. Guard it carefully."

Wally barked, "Aye, aye, Substitute Captain Curly!" He gently picked up the piece of parchment with his mouth. Then he and Henry and the pugs ran up to the deck.

As they ran, Wally barked "ahoy" at another pup—and that's when it happened. The wind came out of nowhere and tugged the code sheet from his mouth. It fluttered across the deck. Wally and Henry lunged for it, but another gust of wind pulled it out of reach. In a blink, it floated up and over the side of the ship.

Wally and his friends stared out at the ocean, eyes wide. The vast blue sea stretched for miles on every side of the ship. Somewhere among

those dark, frothy waves was a piece of parchment. A piece of parchment Wally was told not
to lose, no matter what. It had been an accident.
But would the captain and Curly see it that way?
Wally didn't think so.

Party Like a Pirate Day was ruined. And it
was all his fault.

Crack a Code

"In case you were wondering?" Henry said. "I think we might be in some serious trouble."

Puggly snorted. "You think?" She sneezed, spun in a circle, and sat down. "The captain's code sheet is gone!"

"All right, mates," Piggly said as she chewed on one of Henry's old boots. Piggly was always eating something. "Let's figure this out: how can we get the ship ready for Pirate Day if we don't have the captain's code cracker?"

"Yeah," Puggly said. "The captain wants things done his way. If we don't do it right, we'll all be walking the plank."

The four friends trotted over to the list of instructions posted on the wall. None of the captain's codes made any sense. It was just a mess of letters and numbers.

"Maybe we should tell Curly?" Piggly suggested. "She would know what to do."

"We can't tell Curly," Wally said. "She might tell the captain." Wally thought for a moment. "We're just going to have to crack the captain's codes ourselves."

Wally stared at the captain's list of Pirate Day orders. The first instruction made no sense at all:

STEP 1: DECORATIONS

P	B	A	O	B	L;	N	O
A	A	I	O	E	D	T	R
I	N	N	R	C	O	T	S.
N	N	T	S.	A	N'	H	
T	E	T	J	R	T	E	
T	R	H	U	E	P	F	
H	S,	E	S	F	A	L	
E	P	D	T	U	I	O	

"Pibabel no?" Henry said, trying to read the words from left to right.

"Pibabel no!" Piggly echoed. "Yes, let's do that! But . . . what is that?"

The pups on deck all stepped forward to look at the strange words on the page. No one could figure out what they meant.

Henry scratched his head as he stared at the jumble of letters. "Here's the thing about secret codes," he said, pressing his finger to the paper.

"They aren't meant to make sense when you look at them the first time. We have to try to read it in an unusual way."

"Maybe we're supposed to read this backward?" Wally said.

"Oh, I you tadeepee!," Puggly sounded out. "Nope, don't think so."

Henry didn't say anything. He ran his finger up and down the lines of letters, then gasped. "Look! If you read the words from the top down, they make sense."

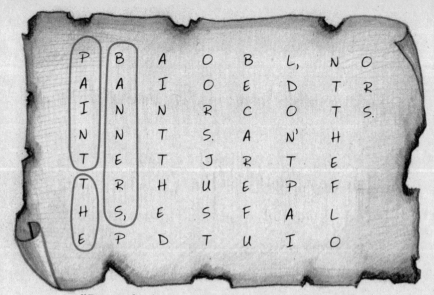

P	B	A	O	B	L,	N	O
A	A	I	O	E	D	T	R
I	N	N	R	C	O	T	S.
N	N	T	S.	A	N'	H	
T	E	T	J	R	T	E	
T	R	H	U	E	P	F	
H	S,	E	S	F	A	L	
E	P	D	T	U	I	O	

"*Paint the banners, paint the doors. Just be careful, don't paint the floors,*" Henry whooped.

"Of course!" Puggly cheered. "We're supposed to paint the ship to make it look pretty. I'll get the purple paint. And glitter!" Puggly loved fancy things.

"Green," Piggly argued. "The captain's favorite color is green."

"I thought it was red," yelped Puggly. "Like the color of his reddish fur."

Wally yipped to get their attention. "The captain is sick, so we can't ask him. We just have to pick our favorite colors and get started. Hopefully, Captain Red Beard will like it."

Wally got the rest of the crew up on deck to help them, while Piggly and Puggly found the paints. Then everyone got started. Wally and Henry worked on painting all the doors on the ship different colors. Other pups rolled out long pieces of paper and painted banners that said: *Yo ho ho for Pirate Day!* and *Three Cheers for Captain Red Beard!* and *Beware the Salty Bone!* So many pups were in bed with the stomach flea that the few who were well had to work extra hard.

But the pugs thought that extra work deserved extra play. And with no one in charge, it was so tempting to goof off! Giggling, Puggly filled her pug cannon with glitter and blasted golden sparkles all over the deck. The glitter stuck to the wet paint, making the ship look like a disco ball.

Piggly didn't like to miss out on any kind of

fun. So she dipped her paws in her paint bowl and trotted across the deck. Tiny pug prints soon made curlicues across the floors.

Then the naughty sisters both sat in pans of paint, covering their tails and bottoms with color. Afterward, they sat on the banners and giggled at the marks they left behind.

Wally barked out a warning. "The captain's orders said to be careful *not* to paint the floors, Piggly. Curly is going to be really upset!"

"Eh, Curly doesn't scare me," Piggly huffed. "She's not the captain. She's just the substitute captain. What's the worst that could happen?"

"Yeah, stop being so serious, Wally!" Puggly snatched Wally's paintbrush out of his mouth. She leaped to the other side of the deck with it.

"Give that back!" Wally begged.

"Come and get it," Puggly teased. She pressed her front paws flat, poked her rear end up in the air, and wagged her tail. "Wanna play chase?"

Wally knew he should keep working. But chase was his *favorite*. He couldn't resist. Puggly dashed madly from one side of the deck to the other with the paintbrush tight in her teeth. Wally chased after her. Olly and Spike chased after him—and soon everyone was playing instead of working!

The pups tumbled and rolled back and forth across the deck. They knocked over paint cans and slid through puddles of paint. Before long, the whole floor was covered in thousands of colorful paw prints, swerving this way and that.

Everyone was having a blast. And then:

Ding ding ding!

The sound of a far-off bell rang through the air. Everyone froze.

"Avast!" A tiny bark cut across the deck. It was Curly. She growled at the crew, who were covered in paint and sparkles. "What is the meaning of this?"

Ring! Ding! Dong! Honk!

"Well?" Curly stamped her little paw in a puddle of paint. "What's going on here?"

Henry ducked behind a banner. Spike shook with worry. Piggly and Puggly lay down to hide their paint-covered feet and bottoms.

Wally panted, trying to catch his breath. "Uh, just doing a little painting?" he said. "These are our decorations for the party. Following the captain's orders!"

Curly took in the orange and yellow ship

rails, the floor full of pink and purple paw prints, and the glitter that covered *everything*. "This is what the captain's instructions said?" she asked. "Really?"

"Paint the banners, paint the doors . . ." Wally decided to leave out the part about being careful not to paint the floors. They had a little cleaning to do before the captain was back up and at 'em. Luckily, he and Henry were experts at swabbing the deck.

"How's the captain feeling?" Puggly asked. A drop of pink paint slid down her ear and splatted on the floor.

"He's snoozing," Curly said. "I wanted to make sure everything was going okay. Captain Red Beard is so worried about Pirate Day. This is my chance to show him he can trust me to keep everything rolling right along without him."

"Everything's fine," Wally said quickly. Sure,

he'd lost the secret code sheet. But they hadn't had any trouble cracking the captain's first code, had they? He was pretty sure they could figure out the rest of the captain's instructions. All they needed was a little time. "Just taking a quick break for a game of fetch. Want to join us?"

Ding ding ding!

Curly jumped. "That's the captain's bell," she explained. "I tied a little bell around his neck. Told him if he needed anything, he could ring for me."

Dong dong dong!

Another bell sounded, deeper and quieter than the first. The pups all pricked up their ears.

Ring-a-ling-ling! A third bell, followed quickly by . . .

Honk! A horn. Spike hid behind an overturned crate.

"What is that honking?" Henry wrinkled his nose and looked all around. "There aren't any geese on board our ship. At least, I don't think there are. . . ."

Curly closed her eyes and took a deep breath. "I gave Old Salt and Steak-Eye bells, too. Marshmallow has a horn. I ran out of bells. There weren't enough for all the sick pups."

Ring-a-ling-ling!
Ding ding ding!
Honk! Honk! Honk!
Dong dong dong!

Bells and horns rang out from all corners of the ship. It sounded like every sick puppy on board needed something.

And they needed it *now*.

"I'm *coming!*" Curly howled. She looked frazzled. "Everyone wants something, and the captain wants *everything*. I'm just one pup. What am I supposed to do?"

Wally looked at the paint-splattered ship and thought about how much cleaning they had to do. And how many Pirate Day codes they still had to crack.

Then he looked at Curly, who seemed like she had *had it*. The bells got louder and louder. The horn honked without stopping.

Curly wasn't the only one who wasn't sure what to do.

"Party planning can wait," Wally said suddenly. They would crack the codes later. Curly needed him. The captain needed him. "Nurses Wally and Henry, reporting for duty."

Is It Ready Yet?
Is It Ready Yet?

"Captain?" Wally said quietly. He pushed open the door to Red Beard's quarters. Henry trailed behind him. "You rang?"

Ah-choo!

The captain sneezed. He dug feebly at his covers, trying to carve out a comfortable spot in his sickbed. "I need a snack," he whined. "My tummy is sore."

"What sounds good, Captain Red Beard?" Wally asked.

"Sardines," the captain whispered. "With pink jam."

"Strawberry jam, sir?"

"Pink!" Red Beard growled. "Pink-flavored jam, Walty. None of this hairy berry bumbo *fruit* business."

Wally nodded. "You got it, Captain. Sardines with pink jam." He hustled out of the room, Henry on his heels.

The moment he closed the door, the captain's bell rang.

Ding ding ding!

Wally peeked back into the captain's quarters. "You rang?"

"Is it ready yet?" Captain Red Beard asked weakly.

"Not yet, sir. I just need to run up to the galley to make it. Since Steak-Eye is sick, I'll have to prepare it myself." He crept toward the door again, then turned. "But I'll be back in just a minute, Captain. Promise." He raced out the door.

Ding ding ding! The captain hollered, "*Now* is my snack ready, Walty?"

Wally peeked through the door again. "Nope," he said. "Not quite yet, sir."

"What's taking so long?" Captain Red Beard whined.

Wally sighed. Captain Red Beard wasn't the easiest patient on the seven seas.

Before Wally could dash off to the galley, Henry stopped him. He said, "Hey, mate? I'm gonna head up to the main deck again. I want to take another look at the captain's list of Pirate Day instructions. In case you were wondering, we have a few more codes to crack before everything will be ready for the big day!"

Wally barked his agreement. Henry's idea to split up was a good one. At the rate they were moving, they would not be ready for the Party

Like a Pirate Day party. Henry could get to work on the next code while Wally prepared the captain's snack. They made such a great team.

Henry raced up the stairs to the main deck, and Wally ran toward the galley.

Inside the ship's kitchen, Wally found Piggly munching her way through a box of treats while she got a juicy steak ready for Old Salt. She had spilled snacks everywhere.

Curly was warming up a hot-water bottle for Steak-Eye. In the process, a lot of the water had ended up on the floor.

Spike was getting a soft cloth to clean a soup spill off Marshmallow's fur. As he made his way around the kitchen, Spike kept knocking piles of dishes onto the floor. Other dishes were piled high in the sink, waiting to be washed.

Wally tossed a stack of sardines into the first clean dog dish he found. Then he plopped a clump of pink jam on top of the tiny fish. He didn't even have time to put away the jam as he raced the sardines back to the captain's side.

"What is this?" Red Beard coughed. His tongue lolled out of his mouth.

"Your snack, sir."

Ding ding ding!

Wally hid his head under his paws to try to block out the noise. "What do you need now, sir? I'm right here. You don't need to ring the bell."

"I don't like the look of this snack," Red Beard announced.

Wally cocked his head. "But, sir, it's sardines with pink jam. Just what you asked for."

"I want it in my special dish. One of the golden bowls I save for Pirate Day." Red Beard pouted. "Put my snack in a gold dish so it will taste better."

"Aye, aye, Captain," Wally said, running from the room again. He found the captain's special dishes buried under a lot of kitchen clutter. He dumped the sardines and pink jam into a shiny gold bowl and hustled back to Red Beard's sickbed. "Is this the dish you like, Captain?"

Red Beard pressed his nose to the snack and sniffed. He groaned. "It's too cold. And I like the jam *under* the sardines. It tastes better that way."

"Right-o," Wally said, running out of the room again. He warmed the sardines over a fire in the galley, then plopped them on top of the pink jam. "This should do it," he muttered.

But when he presented the plate to the captain, Red Beard moaned. "Forget it," he said sadly, pushing the dish aside. "I'm not really

hungry anymore. Thanks anyway, little Walty."

Wally sighed. "Is there anything else you need, Captain?" He tried not to think about how much time he had spent getting the captain's snack ready—time he *could* have spent getting the ship ready for the Pirate Day party.

Red Beard nodded. "I need someone to cuddle with. Fetch my stuffed duck!"

Wally grabbed the duck from a basket in the corner and placed him beside Captain Red Beard. The sick captain curled around his stuffed buddy, then fell fast asleep.

As soon as Wally was sure it was safe to move again, he crept out of the room. He tiptoed down the hall quietly, hoping his needy captain would stay asleep for a very long time!

Nummer Yummers

When Wally finally got back up to the main deck, most of the puppy pirates were gathered around the captain's list of instructions. Now that the patients had all been cared for, the others could get back to work. There wasn't much time left.

Curly was off meeting with Chumley, the German shepherd who ran the map room. The two of them were making sure the ship was on course for calm seas. No one wanted to hit a storm before the Pirate Day party!

"What's the next thing on the instructions list?" Wally asked Piggly.

Through a mouthful of cheese and bacon treats, Piggly blurted, "We dun dough."

"You don't know?" Wally guessed. He tried to squeeze through the crowd to get to Henry. When he was near enough to see the codes, Wally's first thought was that the next one was much trickier than the last:

STEP 2: NUMMER YUMMERS

20 18 5 1 20   20 9 13 5,
13 5 1 20   20 9 13 5,
12 15 20 19   15 6   25 21 13 13 25
5 1 20   20 9 13 5.
16 5 5 11   21 14 4 5 18   20 8 5
16 5 16 16 5 18!

"Blimey. This code is in some other language," Spike said, whimpering. "We'll never figure it out. Never, never, never."

"Never say never," Puggly scolded. "A pirate can do anything if she sets her mind to it."

Henry chewed on his lower lip and stared at the jumble of numbers. "It says 'nummer yummers' at the top, so maybe this code is telling us something about the food for the party."

"Aye," Wally barked. He loved that his best mate was so smart about everything.

"In case you were wondering," Henry said, "I think it might be some sort of recipe."

"I doubt that," Piggly said. Crumbs toppled out of her mouth. "The captain can't cook."

Henry began writing something on the bottom of the list of instructions. It was the alphabet. Under each letter, he wrote a number.

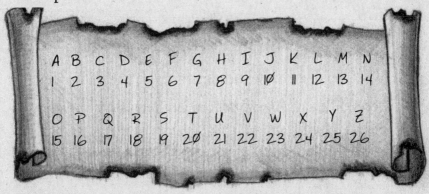

A B C D E F G H I J K L M N
1 2 3 4 5 6 7 8 9 10 11 12 13 14

O P Q R S T U V W X Y Z
15 16 17 18 19 20 21 22 23 24 25 26

"It's a letter-to-number code!" Henry said, slapping his hand to his forehead. One by one, he put a letter under each of the numbers on Red Beard's list.

20 18 5 1 20   20 9 13 5,
T R E A T   T I M E,

13 5 1 20   20 9 13 5,
M E A T   T I M E,

12 15 20 19   15 6   25 21 13 13 25
L O T S   O F   Y U M M Y

5 1 20   20 9 13 5.
E A T   T I M E.

16 5 5 11   21 14 4 5 18   20 8 5
P E E K   U N D E R   T H E

16 5 16 5 18!
P E P E R!

"See?" Henry said, grinning at the gathered crew. "It says: *Treat time, meat time, lots of yummy eat time. Peek under the pepper!* The captain must have hidden our special treats for Pirate Day. This tells us where to find them!"

"Follow me," Piggly ordered. She led the crew toward the galley. "I know my way around the kitchen!"

But when they arrived in the galley, everyone screeched to a halt. Dishes were everywhere, and food scraps littered the floor. Nothing was in its usual place. With Steak-Eye sick in bed, no one had done dishes since dinner the night before. Pups had been in and out of the kitchen all day, helping themselves to snacks.

The place was such a mess that it took a few moments before they noticed Steak-Eye, the ship's tiny cook, spinning in lazy circles in the center of the room. A blanket draped across his back dragged along the floor.

"Steak-Eye!" Wally gasped.

The cook looked at him with watery, sleepy eyes. *Ah-choo!*

"Are you okay?" Piggly asked.

Steak-Eye blinked twice, spun in one last circle, then curled up and fell fast asleep.

"Is he . . . sleepwalkin'?" Spike wondered.

Steak-Eye snored loudly. Then he made a *glug-glug-glurrgh* noise in his sleep.

"Don't laugh," Puggly warned. "We don't wanna wake him. He'll be furious if he wakes up and sees the state of his kitchen!"

While a few pups worked together to carry Steak-Eye back to his quarters, Henry said, "I wonder who made such a mess of this place?"

"I came in to get Old Salt a snack earlier," Piggly explained. "And I fixed a couple midnight snacks for myself last night."

"I got some sardines and jam for the captain," Wally mumbled. "But I forgot to clean up after."

"And I tried to whip up some stew for my breakfast," Spike said. "Not tasty. We need Steak-Eye to get well soon. I'm starvin'."

It was clear that almost everyone on board had been a part of making the mess in the galley. Each of the pups' little messes added up to one big mess. It was going to be impossible to find the treats for the party! Still, they got to work searching. They sniffed in pots and tore through cupboards. Soon the kitchen was even more of a mess than it had been before, and still no one could find the pepper.

Wally sniffed at the air. His nose tickled. He almost sneezed—he was pretty sure he had just picked up a whiff of pepper. It was coming from behind a towering stack of pots. He poked his nose into the stack.

It wiggled.

It wobbled.

It swayed.

Crash!

The whole stack of pots fell to the floor with a loud clatter.

"Shiver me timbers!" Henry shouted joyfully. He pushed aside the mess of fallen pots and uncovered a box marked PEPPER. The puppy pirates nosed the pepper aside. Henry

lifted open the crate below. "It's full of sausages and smoked fish! This must be the captain's party food. Consider this code *cracked*!"

The puppies all cheered. But their celebration was short-lived. Curly had just walked through the door—and the galley had never been more of a disaster.

Old Salt Says

Henry leaped across the mess and tried to block Curly's view of the kitchen. "In case you were wondering, we have everything under control in here."

Curly peered between Henry's legs. "Under control?" she barked. "You call this mess *under control?*"

All the dogs backed away from her. When Curly was mad, her voice could get *very* loud.

But when she finally spoke again, Curly did not shout. Instead, the first mate sounded very calm. "Half our crew is sick with sneezy noses and the stomach flea. The deck is filled with paint. The galley is a disaster. From what I can tell, things are *not* under control. In fact, we are not much closer to being ready for the Pirate Day banquet than we were this morning. We have until tomorrow to get this ship ready for the captain's favorite day of the year. I trusted all of you to help me." She looked around and shook her head sadly. "You let me down. You let the captain down."

Wally tucked his tail between his legs.

Curly sat and sighed. "This will be the first Pirate Day with no party. I guess I need to find some way to break the news to the captain."

No one said anything. It was terrible when Curly was angry. But somehow this was worse.

She was disappointed in them.

Ding ding ding!

Dong dong dong!

Ringing bells echoed from down the hall.

"Well." Curly took a deep breath. "Sounds like Captain Red Beard and Old Salt both need help again. I will tend to the captain. Could someone else check on Old Salt?"

"I will, Curly," Wally offered. "But first, do you want me to come with you to tell the captain about the party? It's not your fault the day is ruined."

Curly shook her head. "No, I'll tell him myself in the morning, after he's had a good night's rest. It was my job to make sure everything sailed right along on his sick day. I must take the blame."

Curly's shoulders sagged. She turned and slunk out of the kitchen.

Wally padded down toward Old Salt's quarters with his tail between his legs. His ears drooped. He felt terrible about disappointing Curly—not to mention the captain.

Old Salt's bell rang again, and Wally sped up. He wasn't going to disappoint anyone else today. Maybe he couldn't fix the party mess, but he could at least help his favorite Bernese mountain dog.

And, just maybe, wise Old Salt could help him, too.

Wally poked his nose into the room. "Ahoy. How are you feeling?"

Old Salt peeked at Wally from under a pile of blankets. He sneezed.

Ah-choo!

"I've felt better, kid," he wheezed. "How are things going up on deck? Everything coming along for Captain Red Beard's big Pirate Day party?"

Wally hung his head. "Not really," he admitted. "We messed up. Now everything is ruined."

"I'm sorry to hear that," Old Salt grunted. "I guess when the cat's away, the mice will play."

Wally cocked his head, confused. "We're dogs," he reminded Old Salt. "Not cats."

Old Salt began to laugh. The chuckle turned to a cough, then a sneeze. *Ah-choo!*

"Aw, Wally, boy," Old Salt chuckled. "That's just an ol' saying. It means, with the captain gone, maybe everyone is goofin' off a little more than they should."

"Oh!" Wally said, giggling. "That makes sense. Yes, that's it. Curly's the substitute captain, but it's not the same. She's so busy taking care of the captain and steering the ship and everything else. There's no one to tell us what to do."

Ah-choo!

"Y'know, Wally . . ." Old Salt hacked up a hair ball. "Bein' on a pirate crew isn't just about following your captain's orders. There's a pirate code, kid."

"I know all about codes," Wally said. "The captain wrote all the Pirate Day plans in code. We've been trying to crack them so we can figure out how to get the ship ready for the party."

"That's not the kind of code I'm talking about, Wally." Old Salt coughed. "*Code* can also mean *rules,* kid. There are rules that a good pirate needs to follow. We help each other out— that's our way. If our captain is busy with other stuff, we've gotta steer our own ship. We need to take responsibility." He coughed again. "Sometimes, Wally, you have to be your *own* captain."

Sneaky Shadows

When Wally left Old Salt's side, it was long past bedtime. Everything on board the *Salty Bone* was silent and still, except the captain's snoring. The rolling ocean waves made gentle splashing sounds as they licked at the sides of the big wooden ship.

Everyone, it seemed, was tucked in tight—patients and all. Other than Wally and the night-watch pups, only Curly was still awake. She was skittering around the ship to check on everyone and make sure things were running as smoothly as possible.

Wally couldn't stop thinking about what Old Salt had said. And he couldn't stop thinking about the Pirate Day party. Maybe Curly had given up on the party. Maybe *everyone* had given up. But Wally couldn't.

He was the one who had lost the code cracker in the first place. He'd started this whole mess. And now he was going to be the one to fix it.

Somehow.

Wally stopped in his room. He hopped up into Henry's bunk and tugged at the boy's pajamas. Henry opened his eyes and popped out of bed. "Is something wrong, mate?"

"Everything's wrong," Wally barked. "But we're going to do something about it. Just like the pirate code says." He barked again, urging Henry to follow him.

Keeping quiet so as not to wake anyone else on board, Wally led his best mate up to the deck. The moon lit their way.

As they crept toward the list of instructions, Wally realized that he and Henry were not alone. There were shadows moving near the captain's Pirate Day list.

Two short shadows.

Piggly and Puggly were slinking around the deck. The two pugs were always full of mischief. What could they be up to?

"Wally!" Piggly barked. She looked surprised to see him.

Puggly whipped her cape. She was trying to hide something under it.

"What is that?" Wally demanded.

"Nothin'," Puggly snarled.

"It's not nothing," Wally said. He drew closer. "Show me."

"You're not the captain," growled Puggly. "You can't make me."

"No, I can't make you," Wally said, thinking about his conversation with Old Salt. Surely the pugs knew about the pirate code, too. "I just want to know what you're up to. Henry and I came up here to figure out the rest of the captain's Pirate Day codes."

"You mean you still want to try to make the party work?" Puggly asked.

"Not just try," Wally said. "We're *going* to make it happen. Will you help?"

Before Puggly could answer, her cape slipped and something yellow popped out. Wally gasped. "Is that a balloon?"

"Maybe it is, maybe it isn't," Piggly snapped.

"What are you doing with the Pirate Day balloons?" Wally asked. He thought back to how Piggly and Puggly had spent the morning popping the party balloons while everyone else blew them up. Then they had fooled around with the paint while the other pups were decorating. And in the galley, they had snacked while everyone else searched for the party food. Wally sighed. "Don't you want the party to be perfect?"

Piggly and Puggly sniffed. "Of course we do. But it won't be, no matter what we do."

"What are you talking about?" Wally asked.

"With the captain sick, and Curly busy . . . well, it's never going to be the perfect party that the captain wanted," snuffled Puggly. "That's impossible without him telling us exactly what to do."

"That doesn't matter!" argued Wally. "We can figure it out for ourselves. We need to be the captains of our own ships!"

"But there are only a few dinghies on board our ship, Wally," Piggly noted. "Not enough that we can all have one of our own."

Wally shook his head. "What I mean is, we have to take responsibility for the party *without* being told exactly what to do." He cocked his head at his pug friends. "Now, are you going to help me—or are you going to stay out of the way?"

Piggly grinned at Puggly, then said, "What do you think we were doin' up here, Wally? Goofin' off?"

"Um, yes?" Wally said.

Puggly snorted. "No way, mate. You think you're the only one trying to save Party Like a Pirate Day?"

"But you just said it was impossible!" Wally pointed out.

Puggly grinned. "I said it was impossible to make this party turn out exactly the way the captain wanted it."

"So we're not going to do that," Piggly said, giggling. "We're going to make it even better."

"How?" Wally asked. "Did you crack more of the captain's codes?"

"We'll leave the code cracking to you and your boy," Piggly said. "Me and Puggly are working on a little surprise of our own. It's gonna blow the captain away!"

Party Like a
Pirate Day

Wally tried and tried to get the pugs to reveal their surprise. But they wouldn't even give him a hint.

"You're just gonna have to trust us!" Puggly said.

The sun would come up soon, and there wasn't much time left to figure out the rest of the captain's codes. So Wally and Henry got back to work.

They took Captain Red Beard's list of instructions off the wall and brought it down to their quarters. Then they snuggled under the covers with the sheet of parchment laid flat in front of them.

The second-to-last code said:

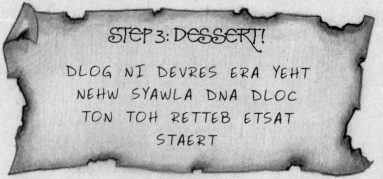

STEP 3: DESSERT!

DLOG NI DEVRES ERA YEHT
NEHW SYAWLA DNA DLOC
TON TOH RETTEB ETSAT
STAERT

"Looks like just a bunch of random letters," Henry said.

Wally stared at the strange words. He squinted so hard the letters started to blur. Then Wally had an idea. He didn't know much about decorations or cooking, but he knew a *lot* about dessert. Maybe he could work backward.

If he could think up some great desserts, it might help him figure out the captain's code.

"Wait a second!" Wally barked. *Backward . . .* He looked closer at the code. And suddenly, it all made sense.

"The words are written backward!" Henry cried, figuring it out at exactly the same time. *"Treats taste better hot not cold and always when they are served in gold."*

"*Arrr-ooo!*" Wally howled. "I know what he's talking about. Captain Red Beard wants us to serve the banquet treats in the special gold dishes he saves for Party Like a Pirate Day. He made me serve his snack in one of those fancy dishes."

Henry didn't answer. He was already staring at the next clue, which said:

STEP 4: FUNSIES

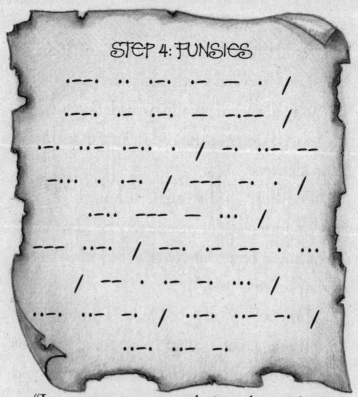

"In case you were wondering, this one's easy. It's Morse code," Henry said. "That's the secret language of navy ships and spies."

"But it's just a bunch of dots and dashes," Wally noted.

"You're lucky I know so much about life at sea, mate! In Morse code, each letter of the alphabet is represented by a mix of dots and dashes. If you signal it over the radio, dots are a short sound, and dashes are long." Sitting up in bed, Henry got a pencil and paper. He wrote down all the letters, A to Z. Then he scribbled dots and dashes next to each of them.

A •–	J •———	S •••
B –•••	K –•–	T –
C –•–•	L •–••	U ••–
D –••	M ––	V •••–
E •	N –•	W •——
F ••–•	O ———	X –••–
G ——•	P •——•	Y –•——
H ••••	Q ——•—	Z ——••
I ••	R •–•	

His tongue poked out the side of his mouth as he thought it through. "I've got it! This one says: *'Pirate party rule number one, lots of games means fun fun fun.'* Huh."

"What?" Wally asked.

"It doesn't say what *kind* of games," Henry pointed out.

"Maybe the captain wants us to figure that out for ourselves," Wally realized. He wagged his tail. He felt like he'd just cracked the most important code of all: the pirate code!

Henry yawned. "Here's what I'm thinking, mate. I think we do our best to make the Pirate Day party as fun as we can. We might not know how to do things *exactly* as the captain had planned, but it will be a blast, no matter what!"

Wally couldn't have said it better himself. And he knew Piggly and Puggly agreed. Wally curled up beside his best mate, falling asleep almost instantly. Being his own captain was exhausting work.

At first light, Henry and Wally jumped out of bed. They had so much to do before the party. Curly was still running around helping the captain. But all the other puppies reported for duty. "We have a lot of messes to clean up,"

Wally told the crew. "And a lot of party to plan. And no one's going to tell us how to do it. So let's figure it out for ourselves!"

Spike raised a trembling paw. Wally could tell he had an idea but was afraid to say it out loud in front of all these pups.

Spike was afraid of pretty much everything.

"What is it, Spike?" Wally asked.

"I think I know how we can fix the mess we made with the paint," Spike said nervously. "We could, um, paint *more* paw prints on the deck. They could lead puppies to different parts of the party."

"It will be like the dotted lines on a treasure map!" Wally yelped. "Follow the prints to find fun, games, and food."

Everyone loved this idea, and several pups got to work with paint-filled paws.

"I'll take charge of the galley!" Piggly said. She led a group of pups down to start cleaning

things up. But there wasn't enough time to clean all the dishes before the party.

Piggly thought for a second. "We can serve the fish in golden bowls," she said. "But I have a fun new idea for how to serve the captain's special sausages, mates!" She barked excitedly. "We can stab 'em with swords and serve 'em up like shish kebabs!"

On deck, Puggly raced around with stream-

ers and bows, making everything look even
more festive. Henry scrambled up on railings
and helped her reach all the high corners. Soon
every inch of the ship was decorated for Party
Like a Pirate Day!

While the crew painted and polished and
cooked and cleaned, Wally had a job of his own
to do.

The most important job of all.

He had to stop Curly from telling the captain that Pirate Day was canceled. He high-tailed it to the captain's quarters, hoping he wasn't too late.

Captain Red Beard was sitting up in bed, looking much better than he had the day before. Much better . . . and *much* angrier. "What do you mean, Pirate Day is canceled?" Red Beard growled.

Uh-oh.

Curly was sitting at the foot of his bed. "I tried my best, Captain, but things got a little out of control. I just couldn't—"

Before she could say anything more, Wally laughed a loud, fake laugh. "Wasn't that a good joke, Captain?"

"What joke?" Captain and Curly asked together.

"You know, Curly, the joke about Pirate Day

being canceled. You were just playing a funny little prank on Captain Red Beard, right?"

"You were?" the captain asked.

Curly hesitated. "I was?"

"Of course you were," Wally said. "But I came down here to tell you that everything's ready for the party. So if you're feeling better, Captain Red Beard, it's time."

The captain leaped out of bed. He shook his body to fluff up his fur. It had gotten matted during his sick day in bed, and one of his ears was pressed flat to his head. "Well, what are we waiting for?" He trotted up the stairs. Wally and Curly followed close at his heels.

Curly looked at Wally, confused. "I don't understand," she whispered. "The last time I checked in, you were all goofing off. No one was getting anything done—"

Before Wally could explain, Captain Red

Beard stepped out into the sunshine. Streamers fluttered in the wind. Paw prints filled the deck. Food was piled high on platters and speared on swords and—of course—heaped inside the captain's special golden dishes. Balloons hung from the rails.

The captain's mouth fell open. "Wh-what—" he stuttered. His voice boomed. "What in the name of Growlin' Grace have you done to my party?!"

Puggy Piñatas

"Everything is so different!" Red Beard shouted.

Wally held his breath. The rest of the crew lowered their heads in fear.

The captain blinked, took it all in, and yelled again, "And I *love it!*"

The puppy pirates cheered.

The captain went on in his loudest, most important voice: "My dear crew, it seems that this year—just like every year—I planned the bestest, most supertacular Pirate Day party on all the seven seas!"

"Three cheers for Captain Red Beard!" the others called out. "*Arrrr-oooo!*"

Red Beard held his head high. "I just love how you followed my directions perfectly." He sighed happily.

The puppy pirates looked at each other. No one wanted to tell the captain that not all of his instructions were so clear. At the end of the day, maybe it didn't matter anyway. The puppy pirates had pulled off a party everyone on board could enjoy. And no one had to walk the plank.

"I have one last thing to say before we get down to business." Red Beard turned to Curly. "The sneezies and stomach flea took down your mighty captain at the worst possible time. But Curly kept us afloat, and for that I must say thank you. Curly, you have proven yourself to be an excellent leader. Someday you will make a wonderful captain of your own ship."

Curly bowed. "Don't thank me for this party, Captain. Thank your crew. Especially Wally, Henry, Piggly, and Puggly. They worked extra hard to make sure the party was a success."

"But you were a great substitute captain!" Wally ruffed. "Three cheers for Curly!"

"Maybe so," Curly said, smiling. "But you lot were your own captains when you needed to be. That's the pirate code, right?"

Wally caught Old Salt grinning at him. The older dog winked.

"Right," Wally barked.

"Just to make it absotootly clear," Red Beard said, "none of you pups will ever be as good a captain as me."

"Of course." Curly laughed. "No one will ever captain a ship as well as you do, sir."

"Yes, yes. All righty, then. Who's ready to party like a pirate?" Captain Red Beard gazed at his crew. "You all have one order to follow today: Have fun!"

"Aye, aye, Captain!" The puppy pirates scattered across the deck. The rest of the afternoon, they sang, danced, chased, played, and ate like royalty.

By late in the day, the other sick puppies felt well enough that everyone was able to take part in the fun. When Steak-Eye tasted one of the shish-kebabs-on-a-sword, he glared at the pugs. "It's fine," he growled. "Kind of clever, actually. Doesn't taste as good as something I would have cooked, but I'll eat it anyway."

"Thanks, Steak-Eye." Piggly giggled. She knew this was a compliment, coming from the cranky cook.

The cook narrowed his bulging eyes and said, "I assume my galley is clean?"

Wally looked at Piggly and Puggly nervously. Puggly grinned back. "It's spick-and-span ..." Under her breath, she whispered, "... now. But shiver me timbers, you shoulda seen the state of that place yesterday."

Steak-Eye whispered back, "Aye. Good thing I was in bed all day, eh?"

As the sun was setting, Captain Red Beard barked loudly. "Okay, everyone. Game time! What game do we have first?"

Wally gasped. He and Henry had forgotten about coming up with the games! He looked at Henry and whimpered. Had they ruined the party after all?

But before he could say anything, Piggly and Puggly trotted to the front of the ship and called for everyone's attention. "Ahoy, mates! It's pug-glorious game time!" Puggly hollered.

Wally breathed a huge sigh of relief. So *this* was the pugs' big surprise.

"Who wants to be the first to try a puggy piñata?" Piggly cried.

Captain Red Beard jumped up and down. "Me! I do! Me! I love games. I love games!"

Piggly giggled. "Step right up." She offered the captain a bamboo shooter. "Aim at a balloon. If it pops, you'll find a surprise. This is our latest invention. It's a game and a prize in one! We got the idea when we were poppin' balloons and eatin' treats yesterday morning."

Red Beard looked at the balloons hanging from the deck rail. There were hundreds of them, in dozens of colors. "Any balloon?"

"Yep," Puggly snorted. "Any balloon. If it pops, you're a winner."

Red Beard shot at one of the red balloons hanging nearest him. He missed.

Wally looked at the pugs nervously. The captain would be very embarrassed if he didn't win a prize. Thankfully, after a couple tries, the balloon burst with a loud *pop!*

Treats came raining out, all across the deck. "Treats!" Captain Red Beard exclaimed. "There are treats inside the balloon!" He leaned in close to Piggly and Puggly and whispered, "This game was my idea, right . . . ?"

"Of course," Piggly said loudly. "Of course the puggy piñatas were your brilliant idea,

Captain. After all, it wouldn't be Party Like a Pirate Day without you, sir."

As the puppies fanned out across the deck to pop the rest of the puggy piñatas and find their prizes, Wally felt so very happy. He only hoped the stomach flea would stay away for a long while. It was tiring being his own captain all the time. And to tell the truth, Wally had sort of missed Captain Red Beard while he was sick in bed. He was ready for things on board the *Salty Bone* to get back to normal!

Just then, Wally felt a strange tickling in his nose. He pawed at his snout, but the tickling got worse. *Ah-choo!* A loud, forceful sneeze knocked Wally off his feet. He skidded across the floor, landing in a heap beside the pug twins.

Ah-choo! Piggly's sneeze sent her crashing into a table heaped with food.

Ah-choo! The blast of Puggly's sneeze popped another treat-filled balloon.

Ah-choo! Henry groaned and rubbed at his eyes.

Uh-oh, Wally thought as he sneezed again. It looked like normal would have to wait.